infamous

infamous

an it girl novel

CREATED BY

CECILY VON ZIEGESAR

poppy

LITTLE, BROWN AND COMPANY
New York   Boston

Poppy

Little, Brown and Company
Hachette Book Group
237 Park Avenue, New York, NY 10017
For more of your favorite series, go to www.pickapoppy.com

First Edition: November 2008

The Poppy name and logo are trademarks of Hachette Book Group, Inc.

alloy**entertainment**
Produced by Alloy Entertainment
151 West 26th Street, New York, NY 10001

Cover design by Andrea C. Uva
Cover photograph by Roger Moenks

ISBN: 978-0316-02507-2

10 9 8 7 6 5 4 3 2 1
CWO
Printed in the United States of America

it girl novels created by Cecily von Ziegesar:

The It Girl
Notorious
Reckless
Unforgettable
Lucky
Tempted
Infamous

If you like **the it girl**, you may also enjoy:

The **Poseur** series by Rachel Maude
The **Secrets of My Hollywood Life** series by Jen Calonita
Betwixt by Tara Bray Smith
Haters by Alisa Valdes-Rodriguez
Footfree and Fancyloose by Elizabeth Craft and Sarah Fain

Don't pay any attention to what they write about you.
Just measure it in inches.

—Andy Warhol

1

A WAVERLY OWL TAKES HER TUTORING DUTIES SERIOUSLY—
REGARDLESS OF HOW SERIOUSLY HER TUTEE DOES.

It was unnaturally quiet in the main reading room in Sawyer Library on the Wednesday afternoon before Thanksgiving. Brett Messerschmidt rapped the edge of her stack of index cards against the grooved oak of the giant study table where she was parked. Latin texts and notebooks crammed with her elegant, backward-leaning penmanship were sprawled out in front of her, as if her backpack had exploded. Only a handful of students remained in the library, some with overstuffed duffels at their feet, waiting for their parents' Lexus SUVs to pull up and tote them off for a weekend of organic free-range turkey and HDTV.

Ever since Brett had come to Waverly Academy, she'd dreaded going back home to her parents' gaudy McMansion in Rumson, New Jersey, having decided that just about every aspect of suburban life in the Garden State was completely gauche. Maybe it was the nightmare she'd made of her personal life this past semester, but she could hardly bear to think about her dad's straight-from-the-can cranberry sauce, and how her mom always insisted on tackling the crowded Mall at Short Hills on Black Friday. The thought of sitting on a bench in the mall next to her mom, eating a buttery hot pretzel from Auntie Anne's, even with bags and bags of clothes from Betsey Johnson and Guess surrounding them, made Brett feel kind of gross.

The creak of the wooden chair opposite her brought her back to the present. Leaning precariously against the magazine shelf was a tall, dark-haired boy with an expression on his face that hovered between boredom and amusement. Brett narrowed her almond-shaped green eyes at him, trying to look at him objectively, as if she hadn't spent the past four weeks trying to make him memorize some Cicero—as if he wasn't a giant pain in her ass.

"*Sebastian.*" Brett hooked an escaped lock of silky red hair behind her ear and tried to sound stern. She'd booked an appointment with her stylist on Saturday, grateful for the impending Thanksgiving weekend and the chance to go somewhere besides the Supercuts at the Rhinecliff Mall—not that anyone at Waverly actually went there. "Focus, please."

"You really want me to pay attention?" A ray of weak autumn sunlight landed on Sebastian's jawline, reminding Brett of how much this time of year depressed her. When you got out of your last class, it was already dark out. "Maybe next time you could wear something sexier instead of, I don't know, looking like Mrs. Birdsall." Mrs. Birdsall was the head librarian, whose uniform consisted of a black turtleneck and a long corduroy skirt, even in summer.

Brett glared at him. "I'm your tutor, sleazebag, not your Pussycat Doll." She tried not to let the comment bother her, coming from someone who judged how hot a girl was by how much skin she showed. She knew she looked attractive in her snug-fitting American Apparel black turtleneck and straight-leg black Calvin Klein jeans, a narrow red belt cinching her small waist. It was a look she'd planned out carefully, in case she ran into any college guys from Williams or Bard later on the Metro-North train down to Grand Central.

"You're not exactly focusing either," Sebastian grunted, touching his fingers to his thick dark hair, as if to make sure he'd used enough gel that morning. He had. "So what. Is. The. Big. Deal?" He emphasized his words by clanking the feet of his chair to the floor and staring straight at Brett. His long-sleeved white shirt looked like someone had stepped on it, the outline of his white wife-beater clearly visible underneath.

"The big deal," Brett sighed, wishing for the hundredth time that she could pull out a razor and shear off his shiny hair, "is that you're probably *not* going to graduate. That'll make a nice Christmas present for Mom and Dad, eh?"

"Let's not talk about my parents," he said, sitting up straight in his chair. His dark, almost black eyes stared back at Brett with arrogance. "I'm going to graduate, so don't get your panties in a bunch."

Brett snorted. "What makes you think so?" She eyed him.

The smell of Drakkar Noir permeated their immediate area and she was just thankful that the library had all but emptied. Mrs. Birdsall had already locked the doors to the upper floors—apparently afraid that some horny Owls would try to hole up in the library over the long weekend, desecrating the sacred study spaces.

"Because . . ." Sebastian grinned, leaning forward, revealing a small chip in his bottom incisor that always surprised Brett. Why hadn't he ever gotten it fixed? "I've got you."

Brett felt a surge of electricity—part annoyance, part something else—flow through her body. "*Look.* I'm not doing this for my own personal satisfaction."

"I know something about personal satisfaction, if you're interested."

He was just lucky there was no one around, or she'd have had to reach across their open Latin books and slap him. Hard.

"*I've got you, babe,*" he began singing. He snapped his fingers as he hummed the rest of the song.

Brett forced herself to refrain from smiling at his lame joke. The fact was, he wasn't taking their tutoring sessions seriously enough, and whether or not he wanted to acknowledge it, he was in real danger of failing out of Waverly. She tapped her cranberry-colored nails (Madame Butterfly by Nars) against the white cover of her closed Mac iBook. They still hadn't gotten to half of the things she'd wanted to cover today.

Sebastian rubbed his hand over his face, looking as if he were as exasperated with Brett as she was with him. "Look, why don't we get out of here? Grab a cup of coffee or something, and you can tell me the real reason you act like you have a stick up your ass all the time."

Brett pressed her eyes closed, thinking of the million other places she'd rather be than wasting her time in the library with Sebastian. Unfortunately, the one she'd been trying not to think about was the easiest one to imagine—cuddled next to Jeremiah Mortimer, her on-again-off-again boyfriend, in front of a roaring fire in his family's Colorado ski lodge, sipping homemade hot chocolate out of oversize ceramic cups. Or maybe, in between rounds of Pictionary, listening to his perfectly tasteful New England blue-blood parents tell the story of how they met. The images mocked her, painful reminders of what she could have had if she'd just been a little smarter.

Because, unfortunately, thanks to her little experimental fling with Kara Whalen while she and Jeremiah had been on a temporary break, and her subsequent lying about it, they were now *permanently* off.

Sebastian's phone vibrated against the wooden table. He snatched it up and frowned at the screen. He answered in a low whisper, "Dude, I thought I told you never to call me here."

Brett crossed her arms across her chest and stared at the magazines on the shelf behind Sebastian. She was tempted to snatch a copy of the *The New Yorker* to read on the train ride home, but she'd already picked up a *People* magazine at the drugstore in town, and right now the idea of reading about other people's problems was far more appealing. So much for impressing the college boys.

Before she could slap the table to remind Sebastian that they were studying, and that cell phones on campus—especially in the library—were strictly forbidden, her own phone vibrated in her quilted black Zac Posen tote with a new text message. She snatched it out and was surprised to see the name *Bree* light up under the tiny envelope. She'd be seeing her sister in a matter of hours—she couldn't wait to change into her hot pink Juicy Couture sweats and veg out in front of the big-screen TV in their media room with Bree. And maybe vent about Jeremiah and how much her life sucked now.

Guess who's coming to dinner? the text read. Brett texted back, *Who?* even though she suspected the answer before it popped up on the tiny screen: *Willy.* Brianna could talk of little else but the great Willy Cooper the Third since they'd met a few months ago while sitting at adjacent tables at the Waverly Inn. At first, Brett had been curious to meet him, but the more Bree told her about him, the more he sounded like a tool. He was a Yale grad, a Wharton MBA, working on Wall Street for one of the biggest investment banks, and hadn't taken a vacation in the three years he'd been there. Except, apparently, to spend Thanksgiving with the Messerschmidts. Brett hoped he didn't mind sitting on the couch and watching MTV marathons all day.

The phone chimed again. *And his parents.* Brett stared at the three words, her stomach dropping to the floor. Guess she'd *really* be sharing Bree this weekend. She wanted to text back, *All the way from Greenwich??* but resisted. Instead, she shut her phone off, eyeing Sebastian, who was still laughing loudly into his phone, oblivious of the fact that Mrs. Birdsall was shooting him daggers from the front desk. Brett tapped an invisible watch on her wrist and bugged her eyes at him. He held up his finger and nodded.

"Later, man." He closed the phone, dropping it into the pocket of the backpack at his feet. "Sorry. It was important."

"Yeah, it sounded important," she said rudely, tearing a list of vocabulary words from her spiral notebook and pushing it over to Sebastian.

"Hey, you were on your phone, too," he chirped angrily, snatching the paper away.

"Yeah, *waiting* for you to get off yours." Brett was grateful to be snapping at Sebastian, because she could do it on autopilot. It kept the tears of frustration from springing to her eyes. Were strangers *really* going to be invading her house for Thanksgiving? If there was ever a year where she needed some peaceful time to rejuvenate herself, this was it. Now she'd have to hole up in her room with some DVDs if she was going to get any peace. She envisioned herself cross-legged on her down comforter, the snow blanketing New Jersey while she ate her Thanksgiving dinner off a plate in her lap, forking a cold piece of greasy turkey and smearing it through her mother's cheddar mashed potatoes, while the discussion of the stock market wafted up to her from the dining room.

Mrs. Birdsall switched off a bank of fluorescent lights and half the library went dark. Brett glanced up at the clock on the wall and jumped out of her chair. "*Shit,*" she muttered, frantically stuffing her notebooks into her tote and throwing on her short black DKNY coat. How had it gotten to be so late?

The whole save-Sebastian project was doomed from the start, so why keep up the charade of even trying? "I'm going to be late for my train. You're on your own."

"Happy Thanksgiving, huh?" he called out after her. Brett wrapped her yellow plaid L.A.M.B. scarf around her neck and pulled on her black leather gloves. She pushed open the double doors to the library and stepped out into the darkening, snow-filled afternoon, too absorbed in nightmarish visions of the Coopers of Greenwich to say goodbye.

RyanReynolds: Did I just see you step into an effing Fiat? Wtf?

BennyCunningham: Guess Daddy's having a midlife crisis. Did you catch the toupee?

RyanReynolds: Spotted that rug from across the common! U know what comes next: a new Mommy Dearest.

BennyCunningham: Nah, they want what's best for the kids. Besides, they have an Understanding.

RyanReynolds: Meaning everyone's bringing a date to T-day?

BennyCunningham: U got it.

RyanReynolds: Can I come?

BennyCunningham: You couldn't handle us. Ta-ta!

OwlNet   Instant Message Inbox

LonBaruzza: Anyone got a wishbone? I have a fucking fabulous wish.

AlanStGirard: Whassat?

LonBaruzza: At the train station now, watching Tinsley, Callie, and Jenny huddle together in the cold. Wishing they were naked.

AlanStGirard: That'd be a sight. Where's Brett? Need a little redhead mixed in to have it all.

LonBaruzza: My fav thing about those chicks is that any sec a catfight could break out. . . .

AlanStGirard: Take a pic if it happens, bro. Happy vacation!!

A WAVERLY OWL KNOWS HOW TO TAKE
CONSTRUCTIVE CRITICISM—EVEN WHEN IT HURTS.

Blue twilight hung over the crowded Metro-North station. The platform was crammed with Waverly students carrying duffel bags full of dirty laundry, eager to catch the last train out of Rhinecliff for the city—and away from the pressures of Waverly Academy for a few short, precious days. Jenny Humphrey let her own overstuffed pink L.L. Bean duffel bag drop to the ground next to Tinsley Carmichael and Callie Vernon, whose slim figures were covered by thick wool coats as they camped on one of the few benches under the awning of the station, their Louis Vuitton and Prada bags scattered at their feet.

"Is it coming yet?" Callie whimpered at Jenny before tucking her chin back under her baby blue pashmina. In her matching blue cable-knit cap and gloves, and her camel-hair coat, she looked like a preppy snow bunny. "I'm going to freeze to death."

Tinsley wrapped an arm around Callie, one of her fur-lined driving gloves squeezing Callie's left shoulder. "If you didn't freeze to death in the backwoods of Maine, you're probably not going to freeze to death on the Rhinecliff train platform," she scoffed affectionately, dusting snowflakes off her vintage gray Chanel belted trench coat.

"I might as well." Callie sniffed, her pretty lips curled into the despairing frown that had been on her face ever since Easy Walsh, the love of her life, had been kicked out of Waverly—for good. Like a knight in shining armor, he'd rented a plane and come to rescue her from the Maine boot camp/rehab facility her mother had banished her to. His heroism, and their happiness, hadn't lasted long. Dean Marymount had been there when they got off the plane at the Rhinecliff airport, waiting to tell Easy that he had violated his probation by leaving campus. Immediately, he'd expelled Easy. "It's not like I'm ever going to see my boyfriend again *anyway*."

Callie shifted her body miserably on the bench. It was just so ridiculous—he'd broken the rules to come to save her *life*, not to, like, smoke weed and play Xbox. Dean Marymount could have been a little more sympathetic, but no, he had to be a super-hardass and prove to the world that he was actually in charge. And why did Easy's father have to go and enroll him in some super-strict military school somewhere in Tennessee or West Virginia or some other hillbilly state? Easy was on total lockdown, as the school didn't allow phone calls or e-mails. Word had leaked back to her that he was now a Blue Ridge cadet, but that's all she knew. It was as if people were reluctant to speak his name out loud since he'd vanished. All her calls and texts had gone unanswered, until finally she got the message saying his voice mail was full. His Waverly e-mail was disabled, and his Yahoo! account had been closed. Her desperate *Where are you?* e-mails bounced back immediately after she clicked send, the dreaded Mailer-Daemon instant replies sitting in her inbox for weeks before she could bring herself to delete them.

It scared her that she had absolutely no idea what his days were even like. Or if he thought of her. Everything on the plane back from Maine had seemed so perfect—her Prince Charming really had come to save her. But her stomach dropped even thinking about how awful Dean Marymount had been out on the tarmac, salivating at his chance to tear apart their happily-ever-after.

"Cheer up," Jenny pleaded, rubbing her striped Gap cotton mittens together like she was trying to start a fire. "You're on vacation, remember?" Jenny looked typically adorable and happy standing there in her tiny red peacoat and mittens. As her roommate, Callie was continually amazed that she managed to keep her energy level consistently at "perky" without a steady stream of espresso in her veins.

"Okay, I'll try. Except they say that Thanksgiving is the worst holiday to travel on, ever, and I'm going to be fighting crowds of cranky holiday travelers at JFK." Callie pressed her gloved fingertips to her temples, already exhausted at the thought of the journey ahead of her: train to Grand Central, cab to JFK, flight to Atlanta, only to have to do the reverse in a matter of days. She hated Thanksgiving. Just another excuse for her mother to drag her back into the South and play Martha Stewart and try to stuff her full of greasy biscuits and turkey gravy. And after the whole accidentally-sending-her-to-rehab-and-almost-getting-her-killed thing, the whole trip seemed about as appealing as a plate of dog food.

Tinsley raised a dark eyebrow at Jenny, rolling her violet eyes conspiratorially.

Jenny winked back at Tinsley, then turned again to Callie. "At least she splurged for first class for you," Jenny pointed out, still trying to cheer Callie up. She'd never flown first class in her life and imagined it was heavenly.

Jenny kicked at a clump of snow on the ground and glanced at the tracks again. It was still almost impossible for her to believe that Tinsley Carmichael was capable of shooting her something other than death glares. Or that she would be trying to cheer Callie up. After all, just a few weeks ago, Tinsley and Callie had plotted to get Jenny blamed for the fire that burned down the barn at Miller's Farm—and it had worked, with Jenny facing expulsion. But since then, everything had changed. Unbeknownst to Jenny, Callie had paid off Mrs. Miller to blame the fire on her cows, not a careless Waverly student. Callie's mother, thinking the giant check Callie wrote had something to do with a drug problem, shipped Callie off to a rehab facility in Maine. As soon as Jenny found the payment stub in Callie's dresser drawer, she realized that her savior was not Drew, the hot senior with whom she'd been locking lips, but her *roommate*. Then Jenny had run into Tinsley, who'd just received a frantic e-mail from Callie begging someone to save her from her rehab hell, and the two of them had borrowed Drew's roommate Sebastian's car. Which, unfortunately, had died on the highway in Maine before they could get to Callie. Jenny and Tinsley were forced to spend the night huddled together for warmth—not exactly something Jenny had imagined could have any positive results. But that first morning when they woke up and discovered they'd actually been parked on the edge of a country club the whole time, Tinsley had insisted on treating them to a gourmet breakfast of egg-white omelets and fresh-squeezed grapefruit juice.

And things had been different ever since. They weren't friends, yet, exactly, but whatever they were, Jenny would take it.

Tinsley tossed her head, her long, almost black locks falling into place dramatically against her dove gray coat. She leaned back against the bench and stretched her long legs out in front of her, crossing her black Sigerson Morrison boots at the ankle. "Cal, honey, you really need to get laid."

Callie gave a tiny shriek and pressed her hands to her ears. "I can't believe you just *said* that."

Tinsley shot Jenny another glance, and Jenny grinned back. She was just . . . happy.

The last few weeks hadn't exactly been easy for her, after learning that Drew, the guy she was totally falling for, had tried to completely deceive her by letting her believe—and even telling her straight out—that he was the one who had saved her from expulsion. But it was all a lie—*Callie* was the one who'd saved her, and Drew was just trying to, well . . . *use* her. Jenny had tried to avoid him as much as possible, but Waverly was a small school, and every time she spotted a guy in a lacrosse jacket, she turned and walked the other way—fast.

On the plus side, she felt a new appreciation for Callie, her true savior. Jenny and Callie had spent many nights in the upstairs common room, eating popcorn in their pajamas and watching movies from Dumbarton Hall's extensive DVD collection. Sometimes Tinsley would even join them, making fun of their chick flick choices, though Jenny had a feeling she secretly enjoyed a good cheesy romantic comedy even more than the black-and-white foreign films she always chose.

"I can't wait for some turkey," Jenny spoke up, dreamily staring into space. She was headed back home, back to New York, back to her dad, back to their sprawling Upper West Side apartment with the super-high ceilings and the peeling paint. Thanksgiving meant cozy mornings on the sofa, shuffling through old records on his vintage record player while her brother Dan spent the whole day in the patched-up leather recliner reading a fat book. She was bummed that Dan couldn't make it this year—he'd decided to build houses in Spokane with Habitat for Humanity—but he'd promised to make it up to her at Christmas.

"I can't wait to see our place again." Tinsley squeezed Callie's skinny knee in an effort to distract her from her mopey thoughts. "They've been renovating the apartment for months, trying to get it all done for my break." She'd spent the last few weeks imagining improvements to her parents' oak-paneled

Gramercy Park penthouse. She hoped they hadn't touched the chandelier in the library, which made her think of a waterfall of tumbling diamonds over her when she sat under it. Thanksgiving at the Carmichaels' was always a grand affair. In previous years she'd met painters and models and artists and writers, including Sofia Coppola, who had turned up one Thanksgiving with a gorgeous male model years younger than she. It made Tinsley want to be a world-famous filmmaker one day.

Tinsley wouldn't have admitted it to anyone, but she actually kind of missed her parents. She couldn't wait to lie in her queen-size bed all morning, the smell of turkey wafting into the room, before dragging herself out of bed to help her mom and Judit, the cook, fill the Limoges bowls with delicious roasted vegetables and gourmet cheeses. Then she'd scamper off to her bathroom—ohmigod, a bathroom all to herself again!— and pamper herself, and finally step, freshly scrubbed and exfoliated, into the dark green Missoni dress that looked like the one Keira Knightly wore in *Atonement*. She would sip wine with the adults, and maybe one of them would have brought their sexy young son, home from Stanford, for Tinsley to entertain herself with after the adults got boring. Yes, it was going to be an excellent break.

A rumbling in the distance brought everyone to their feet. Cigarettes were stubbed out under well-heeled shoes and the air filled with excited chatter and last-minute goodbyes. Tinsley and Callie hurriedly gathered up their bags and the three girls made their way to the edge of the platform in a pack. The train screeched to a halt at the station as everyone jostled for position near the doors. "I can't ride facing backwards!" someone cried out desperately, sending the three of them into giggles.

The doors opened with a whoosh and Jenny and Tinsley and Callie boarded the train. "Wait, where's Brett?" Jenny asked, glancing over her shoulder at the throng of people pushing onto the train.

"Is she catching this one?" Tinsley asked, her eyes narrowing. She'd allowed Jenny to rise in the ranks of her approval, but Brett was another story. Her moody roommate had only been moodier since Jeremiah dumped her after finding out she'd temporarily been a lesbian, and even if Tinsley felt a little bit sorry for her former friend, Brett had made no effort to make things up to Tinsley.

Callie leaned back, searching the compartment. "I saw her in the library with Sebastian earlier."

"She's going to miss the train," Jenny said, alarm clouding her face.

"Grab those four seats," Tinsley instructed, pointing at an open quad of chairs in the middle of the train. "Hey, those are ours," she called out to two skinny freshman guys who froze in the aisle. At the sight of Tinsley, they gallantly stepped aside. "Thanks, boys." She tossed them an appreciative smile over her shoulder as she hoisted her bag into the overhead and slid into the window seat. Callie took the one opposite her.

Jenny dropped into the aisle seat and glanced around, expecting to find a frazzled Brett bounding down the aisle at any moment.

Instead, she caught sight of sandy-haired Drew, who jostled

onto the train with a couple of senior guys, all chuckling about something. Immediately, Jenny's stomach dropped. Surely they were talking about her, and how Drew had almost persuaded her to lose her virginity to him.

"Don't tell me you can't ride backwards either?" Tinsley asked, her eyes focused on Jenny's suddenly ashen face.

Jenny shook her head and reached up to pull off her hat and take out her ponytail, shaking her long curls and sliding the elastic band around her wrist. She exhaled loudly and stuffed the hat into her pocket. "It's nothing."

Tinsley wiggled out of her coat, letting it fall casually onto the empty seat next to her. She folded her arms across her chest. "Doesn't look like nothing."

"I saw him too." Callie folded up her scarf and stuffed it, like a pillow, between her head and the window. "Drew."

The mention of his name caused a chill to run the length of Jenny's body and she pressed her nails into her palm to keep from crying. She didn't know which hurt more: Drew's lies, or the fact that she'd almost fallen for them without question.

"Someone started a rumor that he has an STD," Tinsley said slyly, a smile on her face. "Got it from the guy who . . ."

Jenny burst out laughing. "Stop it." She could count on one hand the times she'd seen Tinsley smile. She wondered if Tinsley knew she was even prettier when she did.

"You know what your problem is?" Tinsley asked, fingering the delicate silver hoop hanging from her ear.

"No, but I have a feeling you're going to tell me." Jenny leaned back in her chair, amazed that she could actually joke around with Tinsley and not worry about her snapping back. Callie giggled.

Tinsley wrinkled her nose and stuck out her tongue at Jenny, managing to still look glamorous as she did it. "You fall for guys you hardly know and turn it all into this big dramatic love affair, like you're in a goddamn movie." She recrossed her legs, smoothing out her dark Earl jeans.

"I . . ." Jenny started, her mind racing. Easy Walsh. Julian McCafferty. Drew Gately. She'd thought all of them were true love—and look where it got her. She'd even almost fallen for Heath Ferro—her first night at Waverly. Heath? Ew!

Tinsley examined her polish-free nails for imagined imperfections. "You just gotta chill the fuck out. Have fun. Don't take everything so seriously. I mean, you're not looking to get *married*, are you?" Her violet eyes met Jenny's wide brown ones. "Or are you?" she added, wickedly. Callie, already nodding off next to Tinsley, chortled.

Jenny's face flushed. "Easy for you to say," she retorted. "You've never been in love."

A shadow fell across Tinsley's face. She tilted her head and furrowed her brow. Jenny worried for a moment that she'd strike like a king cobra, quick and deadly.

"Right?" Jenny waited for a punchy response, but Tinsley didn't say anything more, gazing instead out of the train window fogged by too many bodies in too small a space. Jenny had heard so many rumors about Tinsley she didn't know whether to believe them all, or none of them. In the moments when she hated Tinsley, she was convinced that Tinsley had slept with most of the male teachers, as well as all the guys at Waverly and neighboring schools like St. Lucius. But she knew this was only to make herself feel better about her own embarrassing hook-ups. The pained expression on Tinsley's face sparked Jenny's imagination—had Tinsley Carmichael really been in love? If so—with *whom*?

Jenny settled down into her chair, pulling her iPod mini from her pocket. Well, she thought, anything was possible.

OwlNet

VerenaArneval: So, R U going to miss Alan over vacay?

AlisonQuentin: Uh, we're taking a break, so . . . NO.

VerenaArneval: What? I never got that bulletin.

AlisonQuentin: Just happened yesterday. Apparently his ex is home for the holidays too, and wants to get together and smoke some J's.

VerenaArneval: So? Alan's a pothead. Big deal?

AlisonQuentin: Yeah . . . but I know what Alan likes to do when he gets stoned.

VerenaArneval: So why are you on a break, then? Doesn't that give him permission to do it?

AlisonQuentin: Not if he ever wants to talk to me again!

 **OwlNet**

From: ladygov@gmail.com
To: CallieVernon@waverly.edu
Date: Wednesday, November 27, 3:15 P.M.
Subject: Fwd: Flight info

So you won't forget—see you soon, love. We'll talk. Xox Mom

Wednesday, November 27
Depart 8:15 P.M. New York (JFK)
Delta Nonstop Flight 399 to Atlanta (ATL)

A WAVERLY OWL ALWAYS ENJOYS A GOOD SURPRISE.

Brandon Buchanan tried to stuff his last bottle of Acqua
di Parma shaving gel into his bulging John Varvatos
distressed leather duffel bag, but the zipper wouldn't
close. Heath Ferro, with whom he'd been unlucky enough to
share a room for the past two years, had kept him up half the
night with his drunken, incoherent ramblings about how much
he hated Thanksgiving until Brandon said, "I'd be thankful if
someone would shut the fuck up." Instead, Heath had taken
that as an invitation to list all the things *he* was thankful for,
starting with string bikinis and going all the way to string
cheese.

But Brandon hadn't been able to sleep, anyway. He was completely dreading Thanksgiving break. To be honest, he dreaded
every single break—having to take the train out to Connecticut, to his father and stepmonster's soulless house and his two
incredibly annoying twin stepbrothers, who, by this time, had

learned how to walk and would wobble around the house, pulling out drawers of silver and knocking over bookshelves as his
stepmother cooed about how brilliant they were. But this time,
it was even harder to leave, because he'd be without Sage Francis, his girlfriend of a little over a month now. The past few
days, he'd dreamed up wild scenarios that included them hopping a plane to Paris for Thanksgiving or jetting down to Florida to his parents' winter place in West Palm Beach for a sunny
holiday. But it was too late for any last-minute heroics—all the
flights were booked.

A knock at the door startled him—Richards Hall was
almost empty at this point—and he looked up to find Sage herself standing in his doorway in a new kelly green belted wool
coat, her silky blond hair pulled back from her face in a French
braid, a few strands sliding out glamorously. The top of her
head was covered in melting snowflakes. "*Hey*," he said, immediately feeling ten times better. "Sorry it's such a mess."

"*Heath's* side is a mess," Sage quipped, her wide, ocean blue
eyes staring at a pair of Heath's gray Calvin Klein boxer briefs
hung precariously from a stack of textbooks on the corner of his
desk. "Yours is always . . . immaculate. It's like there's a line
going through the middle of the room or something."

"I'll take that as a compliment." Brandon lightly touched
Sage's waist, fingering the fabric of her new coat. "I like this. Is
it Michael Kors?"

"How did you . . ." Sage nodded, her voice trailing off. Her
eyes flitted around the room, as if searching for something.
"Never mind. You always know."

Brandon hesitated, wondering if this was the moment to give her his little going-away present. She seemed kind of . . . annoyed with him, although they'd stayed out until curfew last night, sitting on one of the overstuffed couches in Maxwell and complaining about their families. It was probably just because she was nervous about spending time with her older sister over break. The sister who Sage claimed had always been the family's pretty and smart one (Brandon found that hard to believe.) But wasn't Sage relieved to have a boyfriend who actually enjoyed hearing her thoughts, and wasn't trying to get in her pants all the time?

"Do you have room for this?" He reached under his pillow and pulled out the small package wrapped in newspaper. He knew wrapping the gift was too much, but he hoped the fact that it was wrapped in newspaper would negate the elaborate gesture.

Sage leaned against the door frame, tilting her head slightly. "Depends on what it is, I guess," she said slyly. Brandon held out the small, newspaper-wrapped package to her, and, after staring at it for a minute, she took it. She tore an edge of the newspaper and peered inside.

"Open it," Brandon encouraged her. "It's just something little, so you'll know I'm thinking of you." He felt the heat rising to his face. Over the past few weeks, he'd slipped sweet notes into her mailbox, sneaked into Dumbarton to leave a single rose at her doorstep for their one-month anniversary, taken her up to the bluffs to hold hands and watch the sun rise.

"I remember this kid in grade school wrapped up his pet

turtle once and gave it to a girl he liked," Sage said suspiciously. "This better not be a turtle."

That's a weird thing to say, Brandon thought. "Uh, I wouldn't even know where to find a turtle," he offered, wondering if maybe Sage had an unnatural fear of reptiles.

"Hope it's your size," he continued, sitting on the edge of his desk and smoothing out his Armani sweater.

Sage ripped the paper free and held the small jewelry box in her palm. A look of horror came over her face, and fear shot through him. "What did you *do*?" Sage asked, her voice panicked.

Brandon strode over to her and pried off the lid to the box, lifting out the candy necklace and stretching it open for Sage to duck into. He'd remembered how Sage said she used to love candy necklaces in elementary school, but had been so sad when she could never find one with her name on it like the other girls. Brandon had scoured the Internet to find a company that could overnight one monogrammed with SAGE, and it hadn't been cheap. "It's got your name on it."

"Wow." Sage stepped backward slightly, touching her chipped pink fingernails to her temple. "That's really . . ." Her voice trailed off.

"What?" Brandon asked, stroking his jaw worriedly. He took a step closer to her, catching the scent of the Frédéric Fekkai moisturizing mist she sprayed on her hair. "Do you have a candy allergy?" He scoured his brain for any mention of allergies—aspirin, maybe, but definitely not cheap candy necklaces.

Sage took the necklace and threaded it between her fingers, examining the tiny letters printed on the candy. "No, it's really sweet."

Encouraged, Brandon placed his hand on her hip, her coat cold beneath his skin. "Just something to, you know, remind you of me." The thought of being without her for four days made him want to grab her and press his lips to hers, but he held back. "I thought maybe you could save the last two and we could eat them when we get back."

Sage's eyes were focused on the toes of her shiny leather Elie Tahari riding boots. "Um, yeah, okay." But before Brandon could say anything else, Sage raised her head, her eyes suddenly filled with confusion. "No, wait. Actually, no. It's *too* sweet."

The pipes shuddered in the walls and let out a loud creak. Brandon's heart fell to the floor. *Too sweet.* He collapsed involuntarily onto his neatly made bed. "What does that mean?"

Sage pressed her thin lips together. "I don't think I can go out with you anymore," she blurted out.

"Because of a stupid candy necklace?"

"No, Brandon," Sage said gently, and it made Brandon feel even worse that she was trying not to feel bad for him. "Not because of the candy necklace. I came over here kind of knowing I had to break up with you."

"Why?" Brandon moaned. "Things are going so—"

"You're just too *sweet*, Brandon." Sage's chandelier earrings dragged down her earlobes, something he'd always noticed. He already had a pair of diamond studs from Tiffany picked out for her for Christmas. Good thing he hadn't put down a deposit yet. "Everything you do is just so super-thoughtful and super-sweet. You're just kind of . . . too . . . I don't know . . . *feminine*."

"*Feminine?*" Brandon got to his feet. He knew what feminine was code for: *gay*. "Because I try to do nice things for you?" How could this be happening again? It felt like a repeat of the nightmare of Callie dumping him—except at least Sage was doing him the courtesy of telling him about it rather than making out with Easy Walsh in public to signal the fact that their relationship was over.

"You're so *emotional*. I've got enough girlfriends, okay?" She kicked his suitcase, rattling the toiletries inside. "What a girl really wants is a guy who can't keep his hands off her, who could just throw her down at any moment and ravage her."

You're insane, Brandon wanted to shout, but he didn't really feel like that. "I guess I'm just too much of a gentleman to be the ravaging type." His voice didn't quite come out as coldly as he liked—it sounded kind of whiny.

Sage met Brandon's eyes for the first time since she'd entered his room. "I think that's the problem." Before he knew what was happening, Sage had stepped toward him and planted a kiss on his cheek. "Have a happy Thanksgiving, okay?"

Right. Like that was going to happen *now*.

 **OwlNet**

From: DeanMarymount@waverly.edu
To: Student Body
Date: Wednesday, November 27, 4:45 P.M.
Subject: Thanksgiving Holiday meal

Dear Students,

Please enjoy a safe and happy Thanksgiving break.

For all of our international students and those without plans for the holidays, the Waverly Dining Hall will be open its regular hours over break, with a limited menu.

The talented staff in Dining Services are also pleased to be hosting a very special, culturally diverse Thanksgiving feast tomorrow, from 5 to 6:30 P.M. Myself and several of your favorite professors will be hosting the meal, and we look forward to thought-provoking conversation about the history of our country and what it means to give thanks.

Enjoy your break from schoolwork.

Best,

Dean Marymount

4

A WAVERLY OWL KNOWS HOW TO SHARE.

Jenny watched the Hudson River slink by out the window as they approached the city, her eyes heavy with sleep. In the window, Callie and Tinsley's reflections were still, their chatter silenced by the soothing lull of the train as it made its way south. The bustle of the first few minutes on the train died down quickly as everyone plugged into their iPods or pulled out their BlackBerries, furiously texting about their weekend plans. Jenny closed her eyes, still wondering who Tinsley's lost love might have been. Eric Dalton, the sexy young teacher from Brown that she'd torn away from Brett, whom Brett had subsequently gotten booted out of Waverly? It seemed unlikely—Tinsley had treated the whole thing as a joke, another notch on her leather Prada belt.

"Hey, girls!" a breathless voice above them with a slight British accent sang out.

Jenny knew even before opening her eyes that Yvonne Stid-

der, a dorky girl from the first floor in Dumbarton, was standing over them. She was nice enough, but every time she spoke
to Jenny, Jenny got the feeling Yvonne was sucking up to her or
something. "Do you have any big, exciting plans for break?"

Tinsley opened a single eye and gave the birdlike blond girl
a cold stare. "That's an excellent question." She closed her eye
again, her long thick lashes leaving shadows on her cheeks.

"Not really." Jenny felt bad for Yvonne, but she didn't
exactly want to be strolling down Columbus Avenue with her,
either. Still, she wasn't about to be rude. "I just can't wait to get
back to my own apartment."

Yvonne grinned at Jenny, her pale eyes full of a gratitude that
made Jenny slightly uncomfortable. The train swayed and Yvonne
grabbed the back of Callie's chair for support. Callie stared at
Yvonne as if she couldn't imagine why she was talking to *her*.

"Because if you don't have any plans tonight," Yvonne
soldiered on, pushing up her wire-rimmed glasses, "you're
totally invited to my Thanksgiving party." She scanned Tinsley's and Callie's faces for a reaction, then, not having received
one, turned back to Jenny. "Corner of Eightieth and Park. Look
for the green awning. Number seven. Nine o'clock."

Callie pretended to fumble through her burnt orange Lanvin
tote, which Jenny knew meant she was trying not to giggle at
Yvonne. She glanced up for a brief second, her hazel eyes scan-
ning Yvonne's too-short chocolate brown corduroys and her
orange Ralph Lauren sweater with the little blue polo insignia
on the breast. "Maybe if my plane gets delayed."

"Yeah," Jenny chimed in, "If my dad doesn't have anything

planned tonight, I'll definitely stop by."

"Awesome." Yvonne smiled at Jenny, her pale cheeks flushing with color. "See you there. Spread the word." Yvonne skittered down the aisle, stopping at the next group of Waverly students.

"Top Ten Things I'd Rather Do Tonight Than Go to Yvonne Stidder's." Tinsley leaned back in her seat and smiled wickedly. "Number ten: eat a live turkey, feathers and all."

Callie giggled and pulled a tube of Stila Lip Glaze in Guava from her bag and smeared it on her lips. "Number nine: spend Thanksgiving with Dean Marymount. Playing Twister. Naked."

Jenny laughed. "You or him?"

Tinsley opened her mouth to reply when her Nokia cheeped from her coat pocket. "Voice mail—someone must have called when we were in the tunnel." She flipped open the screen and listened, a slight frown crossing her face. "It's my mom." Halfway into the message her jaw dropped, and Jenny and Callie exchanged worried glances, bracing themselves for Tinsley Carmichael on a rampage. "Unbelievable," Tinsley barked as she snapped the phone shut.

"What?" Callie asked cautiously. "No tofurkey this year?"

"The goddamn *floors* in the goddamn *apartment* need another coat of *polyurethane* or some shit." Tinsley shook her head in astonishment, looking more lost than Jenny had ever seen her. "So they decided to go to goddamn St. Barts. For Thanksgiving!"

The three of them went silent for a moment, Jenny wondering what kind of parents could go to St. Barts and only tell their child at the last moment. "Look, I'm sure we can get another flight to Atlanta," Callie offered, only half-joking. "Having you there would make the state dinner much more bearable."

Tinsley's lips formed a delicate pout. "Thanks, but I didn't pack my debutante dress."

Callie frowned. "Can you stay in the apartment, or is it, like, quarantined?"

"They want me to stay at a hotel," Tinsley sighed, rolling her eyes. Her face quickly composed itself into its typical, slightly bored expression, but Jenny could tell she was bothered by the whole thing. "Something tells me Daddy's AmEx card will be buying the most expensive Thanksgiving dinner the Soho Grand has ever served."

As fun as it would be to spend a weekend at a luxury hotel, Jenny couldn't imagine spending *Thanksgiving* there. Alone. "Come to my house," she said impulsively, leaning forward and putting a hand on Tinsley's knee. "It's just me and my dad, and we could totally use someone else to talk to."

Tinsley palmed her phone, flipping it over and over, considering. She twitched her lips. "It wouldn't be an imposition?"

"Please. Rufus loves my tall, charming friends!" Jenny smiled. "You really shouldn't be alone on Thanksgiving." She cringed at the thought of her father dancing around tomorrow morning in his Hawaiian print bathrobe, singing Beach Boys songs as he burnt his toast. Either Tinsley would find it incredibly endearing—or beyond annoying. She had a sinking feeling it might be the latter.

Callie dug through her bag, tuning out Jenny and Tinsley, suddenly panicking that she'd forgotten her plane ticket. It was weird that Tinsley and Jenny would be spending Thanksgiving together—Callie couldn't help feeling a bit jealous. Two months ago, Tinsley would have suffocated Jenny with a pillow while she slept, and now they'd be having pillow fights and giggling over late-night popcorn in Jenny's apartment.

It didn't *really* bother her. All she really wanted was Easy. People were already tired of her moping around, but what could she do? She noticed the glazed-over looks in Jenny and Tinsley and Brett's eyes when she started talking about how much she missed him, and she couldn't really blame them. She was bored with it, too, but she didn't know how to make it stop, short of hiring a private investigator to track Easy down wherever the hell he was, and maybe spring him free, if private investigators could even do that. Maybe if you paid them extra?

She turned everything in her bag over, a desperate panic overcoming her as she searched. *Where was her plane ticket?* She'd looked at it when it arrived via FedEx from her mom and then shoved it in the top drawer of her dresser so she'd remember to pack it. But the top drawer was where she kept what her mother might call her "lady's finery," and she hadn't packed any of her silk things for Thanksgiving, with no one to appreciate them.

The corner of a white envelope stuck out from under her folded jeans and she yanked it free. Aha! Callie flipped the envelope over, looking for the opening. It was sealed. She didn't remember sealing it. She definitely didn't remember sealing it. And she definitely hadn't written the letter *C* in a heart on the front. Her heart thumped loudly in her chest as she flicked a recently manicured nail along the top of the stubborn envelope, finally revealing a creased piece of lined paper torn out of a notebook. She recognized Easy's handwriting immediately, and tears sprang to her eyes just because she missed seeing it so much.

> *Callie,*
>
> *If you've gotten this, I'm probably at military school and can't get word out. But I have a plan—I'm going to sneak away over Thanksgiving weekend and get to New York. I'll be on top of the Empire State Building at 8 P.M. on Thanksgiving, just like in* An Affair to Remember, *right? (How's that for romantic?) There's something else in here too, something I wanted to give you but was waiting for the right moment. I think I missed it, so now will have to do. It's a promise ring. I promise I'll see you soon, and I'll be thinking of you every day until I do.*
>
> *I love you.*
>
> *Easy.*

Callie rifled through the envelope until a small platinum ring with a pear-shaped amethyst stone dropped into her lap. She shrieked, jolting Jenny and Tinsley. She pinched the ring between her thumb and forefinger and slid it onto her left ring finger. "It's from Easy!" she cried. "It's a promise ring."

Jenny's doe eyes widened. "Really? That's pretty serious,

right?"

Callie couldn't help feeling a small surge of triumph—despite Easy's brief fling with Jenny at the beginning of the semester, he was back with Callie, for good. A vision of herself in a flowing white wedding dress atop the Empire State Building, the air blowing her luscious curls around her like an angel, danced in her head. She could suddenly feel Easy's strong lips against hers, and the train couldn't move fast enough.

"He's coming to New York," Callie whispered confidentially, looking around for eavesdroppers.

"Too bad you'll be in Atlanta," Tinsley reminded her. "And I think you're only supposed to wear an engagement ring on that hand."

"I lost my plane ticket," Callie said matter-of-factly, holding her hand out and staring at the ring. It was kind of like an engagement ring, in a way. A pre-engagement engagement ring, really.

"It's in your outside pocket." Tinsley poked at Callie's waist. "I saw you tuck it in when we left Dumbarton."

Callie stuck her hand in the side pocket of her camel-hair coat and was chagrined to find the ticket. Suddenly, she realized she was in total control of the situation. "Fuck it. I'm not going." Just because she had a plane ticket didn't mean she had to use it. "If she thinks she can stick me in rehab and then call me home for Thanksgiving only to ignore me while she does nothing but work . . ."

"That's the spirit. Screw the governor." Tinsley smiled mischievously. "Then screw Easy."

Callie focused her hazel eyes on Jenny and blew a loose strawberry blond strand of hair out of her face. "So, how many beds
does your apartment have?" Callie asked Jenny softly, using the
honey-sweet voice she used for calling in favors.

Tinsley's slouchy sweater slid off one of her shoulders, revealing her smooth, pale skin and the black strap of her silk camisole. "You're really blowing off your mom? You sure you want
to do that?"

Callie held up her promise ring. "I'm going to New York.
And that's that." She turned to Jenny, who still hadn't answered
her question.

"Of course you can stay with me!" Jenny exclaimed, feeling kind of excited that Tinsley Carmichael and Callie Vernon
would actually be staying in her apartment.

Did she still have that poster from last summer of Shia
LaBeouf in *Transformers* thumbtacked above her bed? Or those
black-and-white sketches from the Constance Billard hymnal
competition? She couldn't remember, but she hoped the evidence
of her childhood dorkiness could be kept to a minimum. "It'll
be like a giant slumber party."

Tinsley actually laughed. "Thanksgiving Chez Humphrey,"
she said, shaking her mane of dark hair. "Who knew?"

Jenny smiled and looked out at the Hudson again. Her dad
was always encouraging her to bring her friends home for him
to meet—well, now he was in for a double dose of it.

 **Owl**Net

CelineColista: Just saw Brandon at the front gate looking like his kitten died. Wtf?

SageFrancis: Aw . . . I kinda just dumped him.

CelineColista: WHAT? Thought he was Mr. Romantic?

SageFrancis: He is . . . but if he said one more sweet thing to me, I was gonna barf.

CelineColista: No more down-and-dirty for you, sister.

SageFrancis: Ha! Nothing with B is dirty—that's the prob!

5

A WAVERLY OWL NEVER ACCEPTS A RIDE FROM
A STRANGER.

Brett slumped down on the cold bench across from the ticket kiosk, tugging up on the collar of her black twill Betsey Johnson coat. The last train to Manhattan had pulled out a few minutes earlier and the Metro-North platform was completely deserted. Wires overhead buzzed with electricity and a few yellow taxicabs lurked in the parking lot, exhaust pouring out of their pipes. Brett was tempted to try and bribe one to take her all the way to Jersey—but did cabs even take AmEx platinum cards?

After rushing out of the library, she'd stupidly decided to stop by the dorm first to pick up her French copy of *The Stranger* by Albert Camus she'd forgotten—she had a translation test next week in Madame Renault's class. But the trip to the dorm had been a mistake. As she flew up the steps to the platform, dropping a glove in the process, she saw the lights of the last train as it disappeared down the track to New York.

It was all Sebastian's fault. He'd been completely incapable of focusing today, even more so than usual, peppering Brett with questions about her family and their Thanksgiving traditions like he really cared and wasn't just trying to get out of working on his Latin. His Jersey accent grated on her nerves, reminded her of all the tacky guys in her junior high who wore bright Tommy Hilfiger clothes and had pinups of girls sprawled out over muscle cars hanging up in their lockers. Tacky, tacky, tacky.

She pulled her silver Nokia out of her pocket and started to dial her parents' house, but the thought of her mom inevitably saying, *Your sister would never miss her train*, made her hang up, not ready to face the music.

Could she hitchhike? Did people even do that anymore? She could see the headlines already: *Boarding School Girl on Way Home for Thanksgiving Disappears After Stepping Into Psycho's Car. Severed Limbs Found in Local McDonald's Parking Lot.* The world had changed since the aging-hippie AP English teacher Doc Henderson had, as he so often put it, "thumbed it" cross-country back in the groovy sixties.

A horn blasted, jolting Brett up off the bench. A black Mustang idled in the parking lot. The horn sounded again and the window rolled down. Sebastian stuck his head out the window, the cold wind tousling his thick hair. "I thought I might find you here," he said, flicking the ashes of his Marlboro into the air. "Need a ride?"

Brett crossed her arms over her chest, wearily making her way toward him. "Well, you *are* the reason I'm stuck here in the first place." But relief had leached all the anxiety from her body, and before she could think twice, she grabbed her bag, casually sauntering down the ramp to his car, careful not to let her pointy-toe Givenchy ankle boots slip on the slick concrete.

"Then I guess it's the least I could do." Sebastian rolled his eyes. "Could use the company, as long as you promise not to bring up Latin." He gunned the Mustang, and she could tell by the look on his face that he'd done it accidentally. As cool as he thought he was, she felt like she'd gotten to him a little.

"Isn't Rumson out of your way?" she asked suspiciously. She hated it that he knew she was from Jersey—her entire time at Waverly, she'd tried to remain mysterious about where she was from, generally relying on the fact that her parents owned a place in East Hampton to be enough of an answer for anyone. But it was tiring to keep up the charade, and Jenny, Callie, and that bitch Tinsley all knew she was from Jersey now, anyway. Normally, she'd have been embarrassed to have any friends from school pull up in front of her parents' gaudy faux-French mansion, but it couldn't be worse than Sebastian's house. And besides, he wasn't exactly a friend.

"Don't worry. It's all included in the toll."

"And what's the toll?"

"Gas, grass, or ass." He smirked. "Nobody rides for free."

Brett scowled and Sebastian broke into a wide grin. "Just kidding," he said. "You don't even have to kick in for gas. Just the pleasure of your company."

Brett hesitated. The idea of a long car ride with Sebastian on the heels of their hellish study session was as unappealing as eating food off the dining hall floor, but what choice did she have? "Yeah, sure," she said, and walked around to the passenger side. Sebastian leaned over to open the door from the inside and a stale breath of cigarette smoke and Drakkar Noir blew into the wind. He wiped the passenger seat repeatedly, though it was perfectly empty.

"Missed your train, huh?" he asked as he gunned the Mustang, this time on purpose.

Brett nodded.

He waited for her to say something. "Well, all right, then." The Mustang darted out of the parking lot and before Brett realized it they were on the highway, barreling toward New Jersey. She watched the landscape whiz by and thought about calling her parents to tell them she was getting a ride home from a friend from school. She decided she'd wait until they stopped for gas or something, so Sebastian wouldn't get any ideas about them being friends.

"What are you going to do when you're home?" he asked as he passed a slow-moving station wagon.

"Just relax," she sighed, settling into her seat. "A whole lot of nothing." The thought of lounging on one of her mother's zebra-print armchairs, staring blankly at the giant flat-screen TV in the media room, was a little depressing. Ever since her father had opened his own plastic surgery practice when she was in elementary school, and performed an amazingly successful eyelid tuck on a celebrated New York society type, Dr.

Messerschmidt had become the go-to surgeon for aging blue-bloods who wanted discretion.

"And hang out with your Jersey friends?" he asked, glancing over at her.

Brett laughed involuntarily. She hadn't seen her pre-Waverly friends in years and struggled to remember their names.

Sebastian continued talking as if Brett had asked about him. "Me, I just like to get the fucking smell of boarding school out of my nose. Know what I mean?" He ran his fingers through his almost-black hair and glanced into the rearview mirror. He wasn't bad looking, really, if he could get one of those *Queer Eye* makeovers. His hair was too long and too gelled into place, but his smooth skin had a deep olive tone that made his deep brown eyes glint. And his cheekbones—he had the kind of cheekbones you only saw in Armani ads. "Like to see what's going on out there in the real world."

"You could read the paper, you know. Watch the news." Brett stared out the window. New York City was somewhere out in the distance, and she kind of wished she and Bree could have blown off the whole holiday, stayed in her sister's Tribeca loft, and spent the weekend shopping in Soho instead of going home.

"It's so fucking sweet to get away from all the Waverly ass-holes for a while." He glanced over at Brett and gave her a smile that was simultaneously gentlemanly and lascivious. "Present company excluded."

"They're not all assholes." Brett shot him a look. "And you go there too, you know."

"Not assholes, then." Sebastian tilted his head and pursed his lips, as if deep in thought. "Just stuck-up pricks."

Brett giggled despite herself. Of course there were some snobs at Waverly—where weren't there?—but it didn't mean she loved it any less. She remembered how thrilled she'd been when she first set foot on the lush campus, where the ivy-covered buildings oozed old money and elegance. Of course, anti-authority Sebastian had to have a problem with it—or maybe it was all an act, since he was failing out. Better to act like it was a choice on his part than to admit some kind of failure. She turned and eyed him with interest. In the dark, his profile sharp against the window and the lights of cars hitting his face and disappearing, he looked much softer than in the daytime, when he was full of attitude.

"Do you still have a lot of friends at home?" she asked finally, curiosity getting the best of her.

"Loads," he answered. He pulled a crushed pack of Marlboro Reds from the pocket of his leather jacket and shook one out. He popped it in his mouth and pushed the cigarette lighter in the dash. "Want one?"

"Sure." She shrugged. She took a Marlboro Red from the outstretched box and held it against the red-hot lighter, then passed it to Sebastian.

"My best friend goes all the way back to the first grade," he said, rolling down his window and blowing the smoke out. Brett rolled hers down too, enjoying the feel of the cold wind rushing at her face. It was kind of cute to hear a guy call some-one his "best friend." "We still go down to the shore, us and a bunch of friends, as much as we can," he continued. "You go to the shore?"

"Yeah, sure," she answered dryly. "All the time." In truth, she hadn't been in years. She'd spent her last two summers doing the sort of educational programming that would look great on her college applications—six weeks in Crete on an archeological dig, a month in Aix-en-Provence teaching English to low-income kindergartners. But her summers leading up to Waverly had been filled with the hot days and late nights along the Jersey shore, where her family would rent a place by the beach. It felt like ages ago, but as soon as she thought about it, the smell of coconut suntan lotion and hot dogs came rushing back to her. "Wildwood. We always went to Wildwood."

"*Love* Wildwood." Sebastian tapped his fingers excitedly on the steering wheel. "You gotta love the pier, and the beaches. And the boardwalk at night."

"The boardwalk is gross." Brett took a drag off her cigarette and exhaled. "Too many tourists."

"Yeah, but a lot of great memories."

"Not for me," she sighed.

"Why?" he asked, his interest piqued. "Get mugged or something?"

Brett shook her head. "No, you just get tired of passing the same old souvenir shops selling the same ugly beach mats and umbrellas with flamingos on them. It's kind of gross."

"Too good for Wildwood these days, huh?" Sebastian teased her. She ignored him and his eyes returned to the road, the traffic congesting as they moved closer to the city. "Man, this one summer, I'll never forget. I hung out with this chick, Clarissa. And my buddy, he fell hard for this girl who worked at the hot dog stand with her. We were, like, eighth-graders, and all he could talk about was this chick. Poor Neal—"

Brett realized it just as Sebastian did and she squirmed in her seat, rolling down her window a little more and flicking her ashes out.

"It was you!" he cried out, the car veering toward the other lane. "It was totally you."

"Could you watch the road, please?" she demanded, taking a long drag off the cigarette. "*What* was me?" Her only hope was to confuse him. She definitely remembered her friend Clarissa making out with some greasy guido the eighth-grade summer they'd spent working at the Snack Shack. And of course she remembered Neal, with his spiky blond hair and surfer shorts. He'd been her first kiss, and it had been kind of fun, for eighth grade. But she'd broken it off with him after a couple of weeks of holding hands along the beach when Ethan, the older, private-school kid whose father owned the Snack Shack, started hanging around, flirting with her and calling her "Beautiful."

"God, I knew you were familiar, but I thought it was just from around school, you know?" He glanced over at Brett, examining her with an intensity that made her nervous, and not just because it meant his eyes were off the road. "Your hair wasn't so red then, right? Shit, you had those tight little yellow T-shirts you all wore. With like a giant smiling hot dog on it."

Brett gripped the passenger door with her right hand, trying to keep her cool. She faked a yawn, trying not to think of the vaguely pornographic smiling hot dog T-shirt still lying in the bottom drawer of her bureau at home. "I worry for your sanity sometimes."

"I thought Clarissa's friend's name was L-something." His brow wrinkled. "Like, Leona? No, wait . . . Lenore. It was totally Lenore. Wow."

"Interesting. Since my name is Brett." She hoped he couldn't see how red her face had become. Lenore was her middle name, and she'd spent that whole summer making everyone call her that because she was tired of having a boy's name. She flicked the cigarette butt out the window, then rolled the glass up.

"Hey, if you're telling me that it wasn't you, then it wasn't you," he said, flipping through the radio stations. "But you're totally lying. Wait until I tell Neal."

"You get together with him for Thanksgiving, do you?" Brett was desperate for any other subject.

Sebastian shook his head. "Nah, Christmas. Thanksgiving is a bust. It's just me and my old man watching football, mostly. The occasional kegger. But hey, it beats being at school."

A Springsteen song started up and Sebastian cranked it. "The Boss," he said as he tossed his butt out the window. "Excellent."

Brett rolled her eyes. "Can you turn it down?" She pressed her hands to her ears.

"What?" he asked incredulously.

"Turn it down, or off," she yelled over the music.

"No way!" Sebastian banged his fists on the steering wheel. "No way you're asking me to turn down the Boss."

Brett reached for the knob and snapped it off. "Not asking, really," she said.

Sebastian shook his head. "I don't know what your problem is, Lenore."

"Do I have to have a problem just because I think Bruce Springsteen is overrated? And old?" Her voice was withering, but it didn't get a rise out of Sebastian. He just shook his head sadly and turned the radio back on, quickly switching it to another station.

"There's Jersey in you somewhere," he said, "as much as you try to deny it."

From: YvonneStidder@waverly.edu
To: Undisclosed Recipients
Date: Wednesday, November 27, 6:45 P.M.
Subject: Pre–Turkey Day party!!

Hi everyone,

Just a reminder about the party tonight at my place. The 'rents are in London, so we're really going to light it up! The liquor of the night is Turkey Hill rum, but feel free to bring anything else. We'll have bobbing for apples, pin-the-thong-on-the-turkey, and other fun games!

I think I included everyone I ran into on the train, but if I left anyone out, it was inadvertent, so invite whoever you want. There's plenty of room!

80th and Park, #7—Google map attached. Nine o'clock. See you then!!

Xoxo,

Yvonne

6

THE WAY TO A WAVERLY BOY'S HEART IS
THROUGH HIS . . .

Brandon sat on his bed, staring into his open suitcase full of shit he'd packed for a stupid weekend at home. His entire Dr. Brandt skin care line, from the exfoliating cleanser to the poreless purifying toner to the vitamin C overnight moisturizer. His Acqua di Parma shaving set that came in its own leather zipper case. Sage's words—*You're too feminine*—burned in his brain and it was all he could do to keep from nodding in agreement. She'd pretty much called him gay. Maybe he was.

Well, not in *that* way, not that there was anything wrong with that. He certainly didn't want to go around kissing guys or anything, but it wasn't the first time someone suggested he was gay because of his need for beauty products, his designer clothes, his obsessive neatness. He knew he wasn't really gay, but it hurt him that the girl he was totally crazy about could just lash out at him

like that. Sage Francis. She'd seemed so . . . perfect. She'd said
she *loved* getting the sweet little messages he left in her mailbox
or stuck in her bio textbook when she wasn't looking. It had all
been a lie, apparently. Sage couldn't wait for Brandon to grow a
pair and throw her onto the ground like a caveman.

"Dude."

Brandon hadn't noticed Heath enter the room. He looked up
to see his roommate in his quilted Ben Sherman bomber jacket, a
bright red knit cap pulled down over his ears. "You're still here?

"What's up with you?" Heath said, resting his hands on his
hips. "Are you listening to Natalie fucking Merchant again?"

"It's Lucinda Williams, shithead." Brandon quickly zipped
up his duffel bag before Heath could make some wisecrack
about his "beauty regimen." "Sage and I just broke up, all
right?" Brandon confessed.

"Hells, yeah!" Heath held up his gloved hand. "High five.
Single again."

Brandon kept his hands in his pockets. "No, she broke up
with *me*."

Heath dropped his hand to his side. "Oh, well, sorry then,
dude. That sucks. Happy Thanksgiving, though, right?"

Brandon knew this was the best Heath had to offer in the
consolation department, so he accepted it. "Yeah, thanks."

"What did she say?" Heath asked. He plopped down on his
unmade bed, pulling off his snow-covered hat and shaking out
his shaggy, dirty blond (as in dirty and blond) hair.

Brandon's pulse quickened. No way could he utter Sage's
words in front of Heath, who would mercilessly repeat them for

the rest of Brandon's existence. He could imagine coming back for a Waverly reunion twenty years on and having a balding Heath walk up to him and ask, "You still too gay?" Or worse.

"I don't know, man." He tried to sound annoyed. "Just a bunch of girl shit." Heath nodded wisely.

Alan St. Girard popped his head in the door, reeking of marijuana. "Later, ladies," he said, his eyes red and puffy. "Gobble, gobble."

"Cock-a-motherfucking-doodle to you!" Heath called back, but Alan had disappeared down the hall with his bag. "Dude," Heath addressed Brandon, unzipping his jacket and leaning back against his pillow. "Chicks. I get it. They don't know what they want. And if they say they do, they're lying."

"I thought things were going fine." Brandon was a little surprised to be opening up to Heath, who was about as sensitive as a freight train. But Heath Ferro, despite his many, many shortcomings, had been the victim of a harsh rejection just a few short weeks ago, when Kara Whalen, with whom he had been uncharacteristically enamored, had dumped him on his ass. Brandon had actually seen Heath cry, something he almost wished he'd gotten on camera, just so he could threaten to upload it on YouTube the next time Heath tried to walk around their room in those ripped boxers that barely covered his parts.

Health bolted upright. "I've got an idea."

"If it's that thing about stealing a pair of panties from every girl on campus and making a giant parachute again, I'm not interested." Brandon heaved his duffel bag to the floor.

"We *could* do that," Heath said excitedly, "or we could do

something ten times cooler." He smiled, waiting for Brandon to guess, but Brandon just stared at him, arms crossed over his chest. "Let's stay here for Thanksgiving."

Brandon let out a snort. "Yeah, of course. We'll stay here for Thanksgiving. And what? Go to the international students' dinner? I heard there's gonna be charades."

"Will you just listen?" Heath begged. It clearly drove him crazy that Brandon didn't appreciate his particular brand of brilliance.

"I'm listening." Brandon shook his head as he searched for the number for the private car that was supposed to pick him up soon. "I'm just not believing what I'm hearing."

"What if I gave you two choices for Thanksgiving break?" Heath ventured. "You could either A) spend it with your boring family—no offense, mine's boring too—or B) stay here and have hot Swedish sex all weekend long?"

"But you're not Swedish," Brandon smirked.

"Hardee hardee hah." Heath made the horsy face Brandon hated only second to his whinnying. "But the Dunderdorf twins are!"

"The who?"

"Dude, do you even *go* here?" Heath bundled up a stinky soccer practice T-shirt from the pile next to his bed and chucked it at Brandon.

"Yeah, yeah." Brandon ducked out of the way. "I'm listening. The Dusseldorf twins. What about them?"

"Dunderdorf, dickhead," Heath corrected him. "Mr. Dunderdorf's twin daughters."

"Our freshman German teacher?" Brandon asked, remembering unpleasant days listening to the ancient Dunderdorf read from his fat, equally ancient volume of Goethe, stopping at irregular intervals to point at students and ask them to translate the last sentence. He remembered not believing the teacher's handlebar mustache and wondering vaguely if it was against Waverly's dress code. "Isn't he, like, seventy-eight?"

"Bingo," Heath said excitedly. "He's on, like, his third wife, who's, like, Swedish. . . ."

"If only my father could get to his third wife already, then I wouldn't mind going home." Brandon leaned back against his headboard and stared at Heath's *Scarface* poster, wondering if anyone had ever told Al Pacino that he was "too gay." Doubtful.

Heath ignored him. "And now they've got these two gorgeous teenage twin daughters. They go to Le Rosey in Switzerland, some girls' finishing school. Spend the whole year yodeling and learning how to tie corsets, or some shit like that." Heath's voice gained momentum as he continued his description. "Anyway, they come back every Thanksgiving, and the rumor is, Teague Williams hooked up with both over Thanksgiving last year—*at the same time*."

Brandon shook his head. "Only you would believe something like that."

"I believe it to be true," Heath said solemnly, crossing himself. "And if you won't stick around and help me find out, well, that's on you."

Brandon sighed. Heath had momentarily taken his mind

off Sage, whose heartless timing had threatened to consign Thanksgiving to an uninterrupted stream of self-pity, punctuated by a bland turkey dinner prepared by his stepmother and her even-more-hellish mother, who, along with his worshipping father, would sit and stare in awe as the twins mashed squash into their hair and stuffed broccoli up their noses.

"C'mon, dude," Heath begged, "Swiss Misses. When will you ever be presented with this opportunity again?"

"Next Thanksgiving, apparently," Brandon scoffed. "And I thought you said they were Swedish."

"Swedish, Swiss, same thing," Heath said. "It all spells H-O-R-N-Y. Guaranteed."

Brandon looked at his packed bag. Even if he didn't exactly believe everything Heath was saying, the alternative was much, much worse. "Okay, I'll stay."

"That's what I'm talking about!" Heath yelled. He held his hand out and Brandon slapped it, his skin stinging as he unpacked his bag. "Look, bro, it's about time you just relaxed and let me take care of things. I know *exactly* what I'm doing."

Coming from someone who wore his boxer shorts three times before washing them but still managed to hook up with girls, Brandon wondered if maybe he did.

A GOOD WAVERLY OWL IS NEVER ASHAMED OF

HER FATHER.

Jenny Humphrey stalked down the hallway of her Upper
West Side apartment building, grateful to be inside familiar walls and out of the freezing-cold November night. It
had taken the three girls half an hour to catch a cab outside
Grand Central station—everyone in the world, apparently, was
arriving in New York for the holiday. She was too happy to be
home to be self-conscious about the yellowed molding and the
smell of Mrs. Ullstrup's two schnauzers next door. One of the hall
lights was out, casting a dim shadow in front of apartment 9D.
"This is it," Jenny exhaled, dropping her heavy bag at her feet.

"I knew a girl who lived in this building." Tinsley peeked
out the hall window at the traffic jam on West End Avenue.

Jenny waited for the cutting punch line—*And she was a
skank.* Or, *And she always dressed like she was going to the circus*—
but thankfully none came. Her nerves were on edge since she'd

invited both Tinsley and Callie to spend Thanksgiving with her, though she ultimately hoped the holiday would bring the three of them closer together. As cool as it was that the three of them had been hanging out, she kept holding her breath, waiting for the next incident or guy-fight that would make the other two turn on her. She slipped the key in the lock and turned, but the lock held. "What the—" She jiggled the knob.

"Old man changed the locks on you?" Tinsley giggled. "Maybe he has a girlfriend and he wanted some privacy."

"Ew." Callie sighed, staring up at a cobweb over the door.

Jenny turned the key again and again the lock wouldn't give. The locks began to click from the inside and Jenny pulled away. The door opened a crack and the pungent odor of patchouli wafted out of the apartment.

"Hello?" Jenny asked tentatively. "Dad?"

The door swung open and a bald woman in a resplendent orange robe opened her arms. "Welcome to our feast."

Jenny felt her jaw completely drop. "Um, where's my dad?" Could he really have a new girlfriend? Rufus had weird taste, but this was beyond weird. Had he somehow been evicted and neglected to tell her?

"Oh, child, you must be Jennifer," the woman said, clasping her hands together as if in prayer. "And these must be your sisters."

"We're not related, actually." Tinsley smiled sweetly, rubbing her gloved palms together. She was clearly enjoying the scene.

Callie stared in disbelief and Jenny felt all the blood rush to her head. From inside the apartment, they heard voices quietly chanting: "*Hare Krishna Hare Krishna Krishna Hare Hare . . .*"

Jenny peered around the woman and saw that her old, familiar apartment, where she'd grown up, taken her first steps, watched Saturday morning cartoons, was filled with other bald men and women, all dressed in the flaming orange robes. Everywhere—sitting on her couch, in her dad's patched leather recliner, on the blue velvet armchair by the window where she liked to read. What the hell was going on?

Finally, Rufus Humphrey pushed his way through the bald dancing freaks from the back of the room. He was dressed in his familiar moth-eaten yellow pullover with an old pair of Dan's black sweatpants that were about six sizes too small. His wiry gray hair was tied back with a garbage tie. "Honey-pie! You're here."

"Hi, Dad." Jenny's father scooped her up in a bear hug while the woman in the doorway sauntered back to the packed front room.

"What . . . what is this?" Jenny hissed. "Who are these people?"

"And you brought friends!" Rufus exclaimed in delight, holding his arms open to welcome Tinsley and Callie, who were cowering in the hallway. They each gave Rufus a perfunctory hug and then retreated. "They're even more stunning than you described them."

"Dad," Jenny said sternly, standing between him and her friends before he could start telling Callie her hair was pre-

Raphaelite and that Tinsley's eyes looked like grape gumdrops. "What is all this?"

"I told you about this, Smoochie," Rufus answered playfully, putting his large paw on Jenny's shoulder and squeezing.

"Dad." Jenny often got annoyed with her father, but now she was just furious. "I would remember if you told me that twenty chanting bald people would be in our apartment when I got home." She lowered her voice on the word *bald*, in case any of them were listening.

"That's strange." Rufus rubbed his chin, his salt-and-pepper beard much fuller since the last time she'd seen him. "I was sure I'd told you."

"Well, you didn't," she repeated sternly. A large animal darted out of the dining room and into the kitchen. It zig-zagged on the tile, circling the kitchen table. Jenny realized in horror that it was a live turkey.

"You're not going to . . . kill a turkey, are you?" Tinsley spoke up, eyeing the feathered animal that was now circling the couch. The baldies in robes laughed as it ran by them.

"Oh, heavens no. These are people from my ashram. I invited them over for the Festival of Thanks," Rufus announced grandly. "We're all cleansing ourselves during this great festival. And we honor the turkey. I'm glad you're here—you can help share in our vegan feast."

Jenny stepped reluctantly into the apartment and took in the scene. Every bald head in the front room turned and said, "Welcome." She could feel Tinsley and Callie behind her, flabbergasted. She had to get them to her room, where they could regroup.

"We'll be in my room," Jenny announced.

"Oh." Rufus frowned. "Your room is actually occupied. I gave up my room, too. But we can all bunk out on the couches. It'll be like camping." Rufus smiled as if he'd just solved a particularly thorny dilemma.

The turkey ran up to Callie and head-butted her Louis Vuitton bag, the wattle on its neck jiggling furiously. "Oh my God," Callie whispered, her eyes bugging out. She shrank back in the hallway.

"We have to go, uh, make a phone call." Tinsley hiked her bag over her shoulder, and she and Callie practically ran for the elevator. Jenny froze, unsure of her next move. Would she stay in her apartment out of loyalty to her dad, or did her loyalties lie elsewhere now?

"Look, Dad, I'm glad you've got your, uh, friends here. But it looks like a full house, so I'm going to find somewhere else to stay. Maybe at Tinsley's," she lied, hoisting her bag on her shoulder.

"Petunia Bottom!" Rufus cried. "But we're eating at eight."

"It's not a big deal." Jenny put her hand on her dad's arm. "You guys can, uh, enjoy my room. I'll give you a call tomorrow." After a little more hushed insisting that she'd be fine, Jenny hurried down the hall and stepped in the elevator after her two friends.

"Let's not speak of this again, ever." Jenny punched the button for the lobby.

"It never happened," Tinsley agreed, laughing. "But man, I thought *my* family was fucked up."

"I think I have turkey snot on my bag from when that crea-
ture ran into it." Callie examined her bag.

By the time the elevator hit the bottom floor, Jenny knew
she'd survive the embarrassment. "There's a coffee shop around
the corner." She tightened her yellow cashmere Banana Republic scarf, bracing herself for the icy evening. "I need some caffeine."

"I need a drink," Tinsley said wryly.

At Melnyczuk's, the Ukrainian coffee shop with a nearly
unpronounceable name, the girls grabbed a booth by the window and ordered three cups of coffee from the beleaguered
waitress, who didn't look too happy to be working on the day
before Thanksgiving.

"We need a hotel room," Callie said, determined to state the
obvious. "And fast."

She looked up hotels on her iPhone, reading off the numbers
to Tinsley and Jenny, who quickly dialed them with growing
anxiety. A flurry of calls to the Four Seasons, the Soho Grand, the
Plaza, the New York Palace, the Peninsula, the Ritz in Central
Park, the St. Regis, and Trump Tower confirmed what Jenny
had suspected: All the hotels were full for Thanksgiving.

"This is awful." Callie shook her head, her voice verging on
whiny. Her pretty face was scrunched up into a scowl, and she
looked as if she were about to burst into tears. "*Now* what?"

Tinsley threw her phone down on the table, slopping the
recently refilled coffees onto their tiny china saucers. "What do
you have to fucking do to get a hotel room in this town?" she
asked angrily.

"Do you think the fumes from the floors in your apartment are really as toxic as your mom said?" Callie asked nervously.

Jenny remembered what Tinsley had told her on the train. Tinsley's accusation about Jenny taking everything—from boys to life in general—too seriously had stung, more so because Jenny couldn't disprove it. Well, here was her chance.

"Look, maybe we're overthinking this," Jenny offered. "We're three girls on our own in Manhattan," she went on, dabbing at a coffee stain with her napkin. "No rules. We can do whatever we want."

"Except get a hotel room, apparently," Tinsley pointed out, her cool violet eyes staring straight at Jenny challengingly.

Jenny squared her shoulders and met Tinsley's eyes, eager for the chance to show the other girl what she could do. "Let's just see about that," she replied, motioning for the check.

A WELL-BRED OWL IS ALWAYS POLITE TO STRANGERS.

Brett dropped her suitcase on the Italian marble floor of her foyer. Her body was tired from the long ride in the cramped front seat of the Mustang, her brain exhausted from fending off Sebastian's relentless questions. She'd successfully convinced him that she wasn't, in fact, the hot dog girl from summers ago. Or maybe he was just humoring her. The whole ride had been intense, trying to fight all of Sebastian's efforts at some kind of shared life experiences just because they were from the same state. She'd been incredibly relieved to finally pull up in front of her parents' house.

Sebastian had whistled as he pulled into the circular driveway—and even Brett had been away so long, she'd forgotten how huge (and showy) their mansion was. The exterior was designed to look like the Palace of Versailles, complete with a fountain out front where a reclining Poseidon cuddled a nearly naked cherub. "Cool digs," he'd said, without a trace of irony, before she bid him a terse goodbye.

Now, all she wanted to do was take a long, hot shower in her private bathroom, slip on her raggedy fuzzy pink pig slippers, and catch up with Bree. It was hard to really talk to her sister through e-mails and intermittent phone calls, and Brett looked forward to some Cherry Garcia and girl talk. She slipped out of her Manolo ankle boots and tossed her coat into the giant hall closet.

"Hello?" she called out, her voice echoing through the foyer. She was a little surprised not to have been greeted by her mother's teacup Chihuahuas, who usually came scampering across the marble floor at the slightest hint of movement near the front door.

"We're in the parlor, sweetie," she heard her mom call. She followed her mother's voice past their giant sunken living room—her mother had finally given in to her complaining and gotten those terrible zebra-print armchairs reupholstered? Weird—and into the formal parlor at the back of the house that they hadn't used in like . . . Well, they never used it. Maybe once, after her Uncle Chuck's funeral, and once for her prospective interview with a Waverly rep, but that was it. It was a high-ceilinged room that looked through a wall of French doors out onto their backyard, with its beautiful view of the bay. But it was filled with stiff Louis XIV furniture that her mother had bought at an estate sale, hoping to lend their brand-new McMansion an air of respectability.

Her mother and sister were all perched around the circular

table with three strangers, who Brett guessed had to be the Coopers. When Bree had said they were coming for Thanksgiving, Brett had thought she meant Thanksgiving *dinner*, not, like, Thanksgiving weekend.

"Oh." Brett smiled weakly at the strangers. "Hi, everyone." Awkward. Mr. Cooper held himself erect in the uncomfortable wooden chairs, studying a hand of cards he held under his nose. His hair was colorless and thinning, but he had a ruddy, just-went-golfing in Palm Beach kind of glow to him, making him look thin and distinguished in a button-down shirt and crew-neck sweater.

Mrs. Cooper sat next to him, looking up as Brett entered. Her pale blond hair showed wisps of gray too, and was cut into a sophisticated bob that framed her chin. She looked exactly like Gwyneth Paltrow's mom. A pair of small pearl studs—heirlooms, Brett guessed—sparkled subtly from her ears as she put her cards facedown on the table. "Put your cards down," she said to Willy, and he did as his mother instructed.

"We wondered what happened to you." Brett's mother, Becki Messerschmidt, laid her cards down, too. "We were expecting you over an hour ago." Her words were slow and calm, which creeped Brett out. Had she doubled her dose of Zoloft or something? Normally her mother would bound into the foyer and wrap her up in an Obsession by Calvin Klein–scented hug, her giant pink diamond rings flashing, and pepper her with a million questions about Waverly, her friends, boys. Instead, her mother walked toward her like a zombie—in a pair of tapered-leg khaki pants and a navy blue Polo turtleneck, and not a single pink rock on her fingers. She'd never seen her mother, who favored loud prints, preferably animal, and daring necklines, look so *soccer mom*.

"I told you." Brett gave her mom a quick hug and peck on the cheek. Her mom's normally wild Julia-Roberts-in-*Pretty-Woman* curls had been straightened into limp, loose waves. "I got a ride home with a friend." Her mom didn't even *smell* like her mom. Brett took a step backward, almost toppling over the end table. This was totally creepy. Normally, Brett would have demanded to know what the hell was up, but with the Coopers looming over them, she fell quiet instead.

"A *boy*friend?" Bree finally spoke up from her spot at the table, raising her eyebrows. Her shoulder-length reddish-brown hair was pulled back into two tortoiseshell barrettes. And as she held her arms out for a hug, Brett noticed she was dressed a little tamely, too. Or boringly. Brett was used to Brianna, an editorial assistant at *Elle* magazine, looking a little more cutting-edge than she did in her knee-length navy skirt and a white boatneck. She looked like she was attending a tea party at a yacht club. "I'm glad you're here. I want you to meet the Coopers."

"We're going to have to redeal," Mr. Cooper said under his breath to Mrs. Cooper, throwing his cards into the middle of the table. "The rules say you have to redeal if someone gets up from the table, for any reason." Mrs. Cooper ignored her husband, though Brett detected a slight nod of agreement.

"*This* is William Cooper the third." Bree walked over and put her hands on Willy's shoulders, giving them a tender squeeze.

Willy—could she really call him that? It made her think of *Free Willy*, that Disney movie about the fish that gets caught in the plumbing. He was cute—with light brown hair and deep hazel eyes—but in a total WASPy, Brooks Brothers sort of way, his crisp white button-down tucked neatly into a pair of navy chinos. Was everyone in the room wearing navy blue?

"Willy, please." Willy stood up and shook Brett's hand formally. "That's the only William in our house." He laughed, nodding at his father.

"It's nice to meet you all," Brett said automatically, wondering what everyone was playing. Her parents never played cards, except Uno. Brett glanced at her mother, whose dark red hair was pulled back in clips similar to Bree's. Had she just stepped into *The Stepford Wives*? "Where are the teacups?" As much as she rolled her eyes at the collection of purse-size pups her mother had amassed over the years, they were pretty sweet.

A look of horror passed from her sister's face to her mother's.

"Your dad's coming in with the tea right now, sweetness!" her mother exclaimed with relief at the sight of her father in the doorway, carrying a tray full of flowered china she didn't even know they owned. Her mother shot her a look that told her to be quiet.

"Brett, darling!" Stuart Messerschmidt set down the tray and gave her a quick hug. Brett stepped back, stunned. He was wearing a *sweater vest*. "So glad you're home." He gave Brett a smile, but instead of smiling back, Brett shot him a glance that said, *What is going on?*

"Sit down, sweetheart." Brett's mom pulled up another stiff wooden chair to the table. "Relax."

Brett sat down, taking a deep breath. Okay, fine. She would play along with all this for about twenty minutes, and then she'd hibernate in her room for the rest of the weekend, watching E! by herself. "I hope you're not playing poker," Brett joked, resting her elbows on the card table and trying to crack the façade on this new bizarre world living inside her house. She smiled at Willy. "Bree cheats."

A look of confusion came over the Coopers. "Who does?" Mrs. Cooper asked, looking at Brett as if she'd been talking about an imaginary friend.

"*Bree.*" Brett pointed at her sister. "She's a notorious card cheat. She once—"

Her sister cut her off. "Everyone calls me Anna now, honey." She looked at the Coopers. "She used to call me Bree when we were kids."

When they were *kids*? *What, about two months ago?* Brett opened her mouth to protest, but drew in a large breath instead, trying to imitate the breathing she'd learned in yoga. Anna? *Ah-na? What?* Her sister was acting like a virgin priss, and she'd somehow brainwashed their parents into acting like robots. Her mother hadn't replaced the zebra-print chairs because of *Brett's* constant complaining, but because she'd wanted to impress the Coopers, and that just felt . . . wrong. She felt a gurgling in her stomach that wasn't from the milkshake she'd had from the McDonald's drive-thru outside of Newark.

"Anna was telling us you go to Waverly." Mrs. Cooper

turned her pale blue eyes on Brett, and Brett felt them pause slightly on the five gold earrings she wore near the top of her left ear.

"Yes, ma'am," Brett answered, sticking her chin out defensively. She leaned back in her chair. "I do."

"How do you like it?" Mrs. Cooper asked. She folded her hands under her chin, her elbows on the new linen tablecloth.

"It's fine." Brett shrugged, suppressing the urge to say something like, "The drugs are okay, but the sex is lousy." But she didn't want her suddenly nunlike sister to have a heart attack before Brett got a chance to pump her for information.

She glanced at her parents, who stared back at her helplessly. A flush of shame washed over Brett—whatever she had or hadn't said about her parents to her friends at Waverly, she'd never really wished they were anybody but who they were. (Maybe just that they, well, wore a little less safari-print and talked less about rhinoplasty.) She only hoped that Bree—sorry, *Anna*—hadn't made her mother give the Chihuahuas up for adoption. Or worse.

After a painful discussion about the differences between boarding schools today and those in Mr. Cooper's day, Brett managed to excuse herself on the pretense of dressing for dinner. As she pulled a can of Diet Coke from their stainless steel refrigerator, she wondered where all her dad's bottles of Bud Light were when she needed one.

From: SebastianValenti@waverly.edu
To: BrettMesserschmidt@waverly.edu
Date: Wednesday, November 27, 8:45 P.M.
Subject: Back

Lenore—er, Brett,

Thanks for the pleasure of your company on the way home. Next time, have a few drinks and loosen up first, 'kay? If you need a ride back to Waverly on Sunday, lemme know. I'll probably kick off at three or so.

Wildwood Rocks!

Seb

A WAVERLY OWL HAS FAITH IN HIS ROOMMATE.

"You ready for this?" Heath whispered to Brandon, his fist poised against the half-opened heavy oak door to Mr. Dunderdorf's office on the second floor of Hopkins Hall. His face was suffused with a sunny glow that came over him whenever he felt especially optimistic about the likelihood of getting laid. Clearly, the promise of the Swiss Misses had put him in overdrive.

"Can't wait to see how you're going to pull this one off." Brandon guessed it would take about ten seconds before the notoriously crusty old man sensed that Heath was just after his daughters and kicked him out on his ass. With a forward thrust of his pelvis for good luck, Heath pounded on the door.

"*Kommen Sie herein,*" a voice called out, and Heath pushed the door open. Mr. Dunderdorf, in a button-down shirt that looked like it had been stepped on and a bow tie, was shuffling through the stacks of paper that threatened to overrun his desk, his snow-white hair fluffed into an Einsteinian Afro. He stuffed a pile into a beat-up leather satchel that looked like it had been through a war or two. The dusty office was eerily quiet in the early evening darkness. *"Was, Jungen?"* The crankiness in Dunderdorf's voice unnerved Brandon, and the whole plan suddenly seemed like a bad, bad idea.

"Are you looking forward to the long weekend, Mr. Dunderdorf?" Heath asked, fingering the ancient-looking globe set on a wooden stand in the middle of the room with feigned interest.

"Ja, ja, Mr. Ferro," Dunderdorf answered, zipping up his bag. "Always nice to have a break." He stopped packing his briefcase and looked up at Heath and Brandon for the first time. Suspicion clouded his wrinkled face. "What can I do for you gentlemen?"

"Nothing, sir." Brandon stepped backward off the worn Persian rug, trying to signal to Heath with his eyes that they needed to abort their mission—fast. An hour was by no means enough time to search Wikipedia and memorize enough about Germany and Switzerland to gain them access to the Dunderdorf family Thanksgiving, he was sure. If Dunderdorf's daughters were as legendary as Heath claimed, wouldn't he be tired of horny boys trying to get into his house—and his daughters' panties?

"Brandon and I were just arguing about where the majority of Protestants live in Germany," Heath said, rubbing his chin, covered in a slight scruff since he'd overslept that morning and hadn't had time to shave before rushing off to chem lab.

Dunderdorf stared in disbelief, his bushy white eyebrows climbing up his forehead. "Why?" he asked.

"Well . . ." Heath started pacing the room. "We're both passionate about world religions, and we got to arguing about Catholics and Protestants, and we were trying to come up with some examples of them living in harmony, and we thought of Germany. Only we couldn't remember where they lived in harmony." He took a deep breath.

Brandon, stifling a groan, walked over to a crowded book-shelf, pretending to stare at the fading German texts with interest.

"The Catholics live predominantly in the south." Dunderdorf leaned against the corner of his desk. A few sheets of paper slid off the top of a pile and onto the floor. "And in the west. The rest are Protestant." He squinted at both of them, his beady eyes becoming even beadier. "I didn't know you were interested in the history of religion."

"Oh, yes," Heath replied, a serious expression on his face that Brandon recognized from whenever he'd talk about Super-woman or the superiority of the dining hall's chicken fingers to those at Denny's. "But religion takes a backseat to our passion for foreign cultures. For instance, we're both dying to go to Germany. And to Switzerland. Right?" Heath nudged Brandon when Dunderdorf leaned down to pick up the papers from the floor.

"Absolutely," Brandon agreed, his voice embarrassingly enthusiastic. His only acting experience to date had been his role as a thug in *Grease* in eighth grade—and that was a nonspeaking part. "We're thinking about backpacking through Germany and Switzerland this summer."

"Don't hitchhike," Dunderdorf warned them earnestly. "It's not safe like it used to be." The phone on Dunderdorf's desk rang and he answered it. "No," he said gruffly into the receiver. "Can it wait until after the holiday? Fine. Thanks." He clanked down the phone and grabbed a frayed plaid scarf from the back of his chair, wrapping it around his thin neck. He grabbed his bag and headed toward the door.

Brandon took a step toward the hallway, sensing that they'd lost their chance. The thought of going to the international students' dinner tomorrow made him want to kill himself, but maybe the pizza place in town would be open.

"We're also wondering something else," Heath added quickly, placing his body firmly in the doorway and shooting Brandon a look that was the equivalent of him saying, *Don't get your panties in a bunch*.

Dunderdorf pulled on a heavy, dark green, military-looking overcoat from the coatrack in the corner. "Yes?"

"What is the main difference between German sausage and Polish sausage?" Heath asked, arching his eyebrows like a scientist.

A pause, then a smile spread across Dunderdorf's face. "My boy, German sausage is far superior to Polish or any other sausage," he answered, inadvertently licking his lips. "German sausage uses ground venison and fresh pork. Polish sausage is made with pork butt and rat meat. That's just one difference. But it probably all tastes the same to you, eh?"

"That's the problem, sir." Heath frowned slightly, and his eyes took on a faraway look. "We've never tasted a really good German sausage. We're dying to find out what it tastes like."

Brandon tried to hide his disbelief—and disgust. He'd only come along on this dumb errand because he didn't want to be alone in his room to brood over Sage or to wonder where she was, what she was up to now, what her Thanksgiving would be like. Also, though he hated to admit it, a tiny part of him wanted to see Heath fail and get kicked to the curb, as there was no way Dunderdorf was going to fall for such a stupid ruse. But as he watched Heath work Dunderdorf over with questions about German cuisine, including a particularly bald question about whether or not the Dunderdorfs would be enjoying a turkey sausage at Thanksgiving, Brandon wondered why *he* wasn't trying harder.

Of course he'd wanted to sleep with Sage—he'd been thinking about it since the first time she spoke with him. But except for a handful of intense make-out sessions, he hadn't really tried to get past second base. Was he not born with the horny gene or something? Couldn't he at least try to get into hooking up with two European hotties, if only to forget about Sage's harsh holiday breakup?

"Why don't you boys drop by our place tomorrow," Dunderdorf finally asked, his brow dotted with perspiration.

"Oh, no!" Heath held up his hands, ever the subtle actor. "We couldn't impose on you at Thanksgiving, could we?" He shot Brandon a look that told Brandon he better step up.

"That's a nice invitation," Brandon agreed. "We were planning on going to the international students' dinner. . . ." Heath's eyes widened, and Brandon knew he'd freaked him out. "But they probably won't have any good German sausage."

"Then it's settled," Dunderdorf said, a gleam in his eye. He pulled on an ugly plaid hat that matched his scarf and then buttoned up his coat. "It'll be our pleasure to host you with some real German food. Thanksgiving is an all-day celebration with our family, so better come bright and early if you want to truly experience *ein authentisches Deutsches Thanksgiving.*" He slapped Heath on the back weakly and nodded at Brandon as he scuttled them both into the hallway and closed his office door, whistling as he clomped down the hall.

"Unbelievable." Brandon leaned against the wall of the long, dimly lit hallway.

"Yeah, thanks to me," Heath countered, irritated. "You'd better bring your A-game tomorrow, 'cause I can't carry us both again." Then his face broke out into a goofy grin. "But that was fucking beautiful, wasn't it?" He did a little dance, shaking his pelvis.

 Owl Net   Instant Message Inbox

---

CliffordMontgomery: Hey, you going to that chick Yvonne's party?

AlisonQuentin: The turkey-themed one? Uh, dunno. You?

CliffordMontgomery: Maybe. My stupid stepdad's other kids are here, and they suck.

AlisonQuentin: At least your parents don't think T-Day is a colonialist holiday and celebrate by burning effigies of pilgrims!

CliffordMontgomery: Whoa. Maybe Wild Turkey bourbon isn't so bad, after all.

AlisonQuentin: Save one for me.

OwlNet   Instant Message Inbox

KaraWhalen: Big bash at Yvonne's tonight. U going?

EmilyJenkins: Bobbing for apples?

KaraWhalen: I'm hoping that was a joke . . . but I think she
                    has a hot tub.

EmilyJenkins: With my pale butt? Don't think so.

KaraWhalen: Heard her invite Pierce O'Connor on the train. . . .

EmilyJenkins: In THAT case, I need some self-tanner and a
                    new bikini!!!

A WAVERLY OWL IS ALWAYS READY FOR THE APPEARANCE

OF AN OLD FRIEND . . . OR AN OLD ENEMY.

As the girls trudged up Fifth Avenue and the sidewalks started to turn slushy, Callie wished she'd worn something more practical than her square-toed Missoni flats. She'd expected to be on a plane to Atlanta right now, leaning back in her first-class seat, shoes kicked off. But she was almost deliriously happy she wasn't—she was going to see Easy again. *Tomorrow.* She couldn't help pulling off her glove to look once again at the elegant amethyst ring. It was beautiful—simple, of course, because Easy was like that, but beautiful none the less.

"My feet are going numb," Callie spoke up dreamily, thinking about how nice it would be to curl up with Easy and have him give her a foot massage. Although, since he was the one going to military school where they made him do who knew what—cross-country treks over rugged terrain, grueling 20K runs, shooting practice—he probably needed a massage more than she did.

"Get under here." Tinsley grabbed Callie's arm and tugged her under the edge of a sophisticated-looking hotel entrance. Callie glanced up and read the beautiful script, *The Granfield.* The three huddled together near the revolving door, letting the heat from the entrance bathe them. "Let's focus." Tinsley eyed the two bellhops in distinguished navy and red uniforms who kept breezing through the revolving doors to grab the expensive luggage from the trunks of the long, sleek black cars that pulled up to the curb.

Callie glanced up the street toward Central Park. A purplish fog had descended with the cold over the remaining joggers and dog walkers.

"Come on. Let's not stand out here like plebeians." Before Jenny and Callie could say another word, Tinsley breezed through the doors, her Prada bag hanging at her side. She strode, with authority, over to the front desk, where a handsome man in a suit stood behind a computer.

"What do you think she's saying?" Jenny whispered, gazing around at the black marble floor that managed to look perfectly polished despite the slushy evening outside.

Callie moved her hand to see how her promise ring sparkled in the glittery light from the chandelier above them. "Dunno," she answered, absently. "Just hope it works." They watched with amusement as Tinsley did her best Marilyn Monroe impression, batting her doe eyes and flirting with the clerk.

"I know you always have an extra room set aside in case

Madonna or someone pops in. Don't you know who *she* is?"
She pointed at Callie, who smiled weakly. After an hour of
trudging around in the slushy New York weather, Callie's hair
was mashed against her forehead. She probably looked like the
Bride of Frankenstein.

"No." The clerk glanced over Tinsley's shoulder at the
woman in a fur coat who was approaching the desk.

"Well, she's the *governor* of *Georgia's* daughter." Tinsley smiled
triumphantly, her pearly white teeth like an ad for toothpaste.
"Now could we get a room, please?"

"Sweetheart, we just don't *have* any rooms." The clerk shook
his head impatiently. "We're booked months in advance for this
weekend. Even Madonna couldn't get a room tonight."

"I doubt that." Tinsley spun on her heel. "You should be
expecting a letter from the governor soon." She turned to Jenny
and Callie and said, "I *had* to get the gay clerk." They followed
Tinsley back out onto the street. "Fuck."

Jenny let out a soft sigh. "I mean . . . we could always go
back to my dad's. . . ." She trailed off when Tinsley shot her a
dark look.

"Let's grab a cab to the Peninsula. I'm going to have to
change our 'governor's daughter' story—it's just not working."
As Jenny and Tinsley strode purposefully toward Madison
Avenue, Callie stopped in her tracks, her eyes looking up to
meet the most beautiful white dress she'd ever seen—an A-line
gown with draped bustling and a bronze antique mesh ribbon
at the empire waist. It was a sign—it *had* to be a sign. Her eyes
floated upward to the Vera Wang decal above the door.

Callie imagined herself wearing the gauzy dress as she rode the elevator to the top of the Empire State Building to meet Easy. The image was perfect, like a wedding cake. She pushed on the door to the boutique, but the door caught just as the lights dimmed. The store was closed for the night.

Callie fumbled through her Lanvin tote for her crushed package of Marlboro Ultra Lights and kept staring at the dress. It was just so perfect.

"Wait a second." Jenny exclaimed, putting a mittened hand on Tinsley's arm before she could hail a cab. "Look where we are."

Tinsley glanced up and down Madison. "Stranded?"

"Yeah." Jenny rolled her eyes. "And who do we know on the Upper East Side who so graciously invited us to her parent-free house tonight?"

"Do we have a choice?" Tinsley asked miserably. That nerdy British girl? Well, Yvonne Stidder's was better than being on the street, so long as her parents had left her a fully stocked liquor cabinet. "I totally need a drink." She spotted Callie, her face practically pressed to the glass outside Vera Wang, staring up at a wedding dress. Christ. That girl definitely just needed to get laid so she could stop with the goddamn wedding planning.

The short walk toward Park Avenue felt like an eternity, crawling across crowded streets, overloaded with their heavy suitcases. Tinsley's stacked-heel Givenchy boots pounded against the city pavement, and she started to feel a little better, even if she was still totally bitter at her parents for so thoughtlessly putting her into this situation to begin with. Finally, they stood in front number 866 East Eightieth Street, a towering stone building with a doorman who looked like an Italian movie star. He opened the door for the girls the second they paused outside.

"We're here to see Yvonne Stidder," Jenny peeped, staring in awe at the giant blurry painting hanging over the sofa in the lobby.

"Yes, of course." The doorman tipped his hat, smiling at Tinsley as he grabbed all three of their bags and brought them to the elevator. "They're all upstairs already. Top floor."

"*They* who?" Callie whispered as they waited for the elevator. "I hope it's not all her jazz band friends."

"I don't know if I can stomach a nerdfest tonight." Tinsley punched the gold PH button.

"At least it has to be warm," Jenny offered, her lips slightly blue.

"And not overrun with Hare Krishnas," Tinsley added.

The elevator opened into another small lobby decorated with abstract paintings and severe couches that looked too small to sit on. Straight ahead of them a door was propped open, and jazzy dance music filtered out. The girls dropped their bags inside the front door and took in the scene: the posh living room, a wall of windows looking out on the city, done up in tasteful dark blues and browns, and filled with sleek, modern furniture. And mobbed with fellow Waverly Owls.

"There's Kara!" Jenny cried excitedly, shedding her red pea-coat and hanging it in the open coatroom. "I forgot she's from

Brooklyn. And Alison Quentin. Thank God." Tinsley spotted the girls on a long leather couch, surrounded by older-looking guys with martini glasses in hand.

"This is insane," Callie hissed under her breath to Tinsley as they stepped around Clifford Montgomery, a senior guy with perpetually tousled dark hair and black square-framed glasses. "Who knew Yvonne had friends? Cute ones!"

"Who *wouldn't* if they owned a place like this?" Out the full-length windows was a rooftop deck with 360-degree views of the city, a solid evergreen hedge encircling the whole thing, and a hot tub the size of a small swimming pool. Splashing around was Yvonne's older brother, Jeremy, whom Tinsley recognized from a day back in freshman year when Yvonne's family had come to visit Waverly. She didn't remember Jeremy being so . . . *cute*, though. Jeremy drunkenly splashed some of his equally cute friends in the hot tub just as a girl in a red bikini descended the stairs into the steaming water.

"I can't believe you made it!" Yvonne shrieked, cutting through the noisy crowd. She wore a paisley halter top that might have been cute if it hadn't been for the paisleys, and a pair of black jeans that were a little too short for her. "This is so awesome."

"Nice place," Jenny complimented her, her chocolate-colored eyes roving the room. "And great party—it's packed."

"I swear, I think half of Waverly is here," Yvonne said, swooning a little at her own success. Tinsley and Callie glanced at each other and snickered.

A pinball machine somewhere rang through the penthouse

like a fire alarm, though no one seemed to notice. The phone in Yvonne's hip pocket buzzed and she flipped it open. "Make yourself at home," she said, squeezing Jenny's arm before fluttering away.

"I totally need to change," Callie complained, touching her damp hair with her fingertips. "I feel all sweaty and grody."

"Thought you were, like, engaged?" Tinsley ran her fingers through her hair, bringing her dark waves back to life. Callie rolled her eyes at Tinsley before snatching up her bag and disappearing down the hallway in search of a bathroom. This was a legitimate party. It just went to show what could happen when Waverly Owls were bored in New York.

"I'm going to go talk to Kara." Jenny disappeared into the throng of people, throwing her arms around Kara Whalen, annoying Brett's ex-girl toy, as the blond girl next to her watched. *Wait*. That wavy blond hair was totally familiar, and as the girl turned toward Jenny and shook her hand, Tinsley recognized her. Sleigh Monroe-Hill, her roommate for all of three months freshman year. A cold sweat—brought on not by any sort of nervousness but rather a very focused anger—broke out across her skin.

Sleigh Monroe-Hill was the biggest bitch Tinsley had *ever* met—and she'd met plenty. They'd been at each other's throats since their very first day at Waverly, when Alexander Zales, captain of the soccer team and the hottest guy in the junior class, had sat down next to them in the dining hall. That was all it had taken: A few days later, Sleigh had told him that Tinsley had some mysterious skin condition—something that caused itching in unmentionable places. Tinsley had gotten her back by shrinking all Sleigh's designer jeans in the basement laundry room, sending them through cycle after cycle until they were all a size too small. Sleigh had moped around wearing draw-string corduroys and eating Jell-O for weeks, convinced she'd gained the freshman fifteen.

But when Sleigh found out that Tinsley had hooked up with Alexander (ah, sweet Alexander) after one of his soccer games, she completely wigged out, tossing all of Tinsley's stuff—clothes, books, laptop, La Perla underwear, boxes of tampons, *everything*—from their fourth-floor dorm window in Graham Hall. Totally insane. Shortly afterward, Tinsley came back from lunch to find Sleigh's side of the room cleared out, like she'd never been there. Dean Marymount called Tinsley in and told her that Sleigh was on a short "mental health leave," but Tinsley never saw Sleigh again, and enjoyed a coveted single—with two closets—for the rest of freshman year.

Tinsley pretended to examine a framed antique map of Manhattan hanging on the living room wall while she glanced at Sleigh out of the corner of her eye.

"Surprised to see you here, Carmichael." Cliff Montgomery, smirk on his face, appeared in front of her. He wore a tight-fitting royal blue sweater over a wrinkled white button-down and a pair of beat-up Doc Martens.

"Why's that?" Tinsley asked icily, annoyed that he was obstructing her view of Sleigh. Her insides were fluttering at the unexpected reappearance of her nemesis, and she could barely concentrate. *What the hell was Sleigh doing here?*

"Thought you only hung out at beautiful-people places."
Cliff shrugged. "Like the Beatrice Inn?" He dropped the name
of an exclusive venue, like it made him cooler just for knowing
it. Cliff was cute, in an emo, Death Cab for Cutie kind of way.
But he'd had a chip on his shoulder ever since an Italian Club
field trip to see *La Bohème*, when Tinsley had let him kiss her
in the darkness of the Metropolitan Opera House—and then
never let him repeat it.

"Would you mind getting me a drink?" Tinsley asked
sweetly, just wanting to get rid of Cliff, and as far as possible
from Sleigh. The last rumor Tinsley had heard was that Sleigh
was being homeschooled and had reinvented herself as some
kind of Joan Baez folk singer wannabe. The leather barrette
with the wood stick in her tangled blond hair, along with the
dirty-looking jeans and the flower-child tank top, seemed to
support the rumor. Please.

As Cliff moved off to procure her a cocktail, Tinsley grabbed
her bag and ducked into the first doorway she could find. It
belonged to a guest room with deep charcoal walls and a low
bed, a door at the other side opening into a small bathroom.
After glancing at herself in the mirror and applying a swipe of
coal gray eyeliner, Tinsley felt more like herself. In her black
American Apparel wrap dress, the edges of her peach Cosabella
camisole peeking out, she looked sexy, relaxed, and completely
unconcerned about any other girl in the room.

Sleigh Monroe-Hill could kiss her ass.

A WAVERLY OWL KNOWS HOW TO KILL TIME UNTIL SHE GETS TO KISS HER BOYFRIEND AGAIN.

After changing into a tan Kyumi bubble-sleeved jersey dress, brown patterned tights, and a pair of royal blue velvet flats in Yvonne Stidder's high-ceilinged powder room, Callie felt much better. For the millionth time she wished Easy were there with her. It just wasn't as much fun spreading her DuWop lip venom across her lips knowing that he wouldn't be kissing them—at least, not tonight. *Tomorrow*, she thought dreamily as she strode back into the party, her shoes padding softly against the wide-planked Brazilian walnut floors. She made her way to the wall of windows and stared out at the city, wondering if Easy had managed to get away from military school yet, and if his plans for a romantic weekend included a suite at the W hotel.

She was so deep in thought she barely heard the guy standing next to her ask her a question.

"Sorry, what?" she asked, tearing her eyes away from the dark night. A guy with short blond hair and a jaw like Brad Pitt's stood in front of her, holding out a martini glass filled with a pink liquid, a cherry floating at the top.

"Yvonne asked me to bring you a cosmo—she said you looked like you could use one." He offered the drink to her, and she took it, eyeing him up and down. He wore a fitted gray Hugo Boss sweater over a blue dress shirt and a pair of dark Rock & Republic jeans—exactly the kind of outfit she would have picked out for Easy, if only Easy would let her pick out his clothes.

Callie smiled, kind of grateful that she'd gone the extra step with the lip gloss anyway. "Well, thank you," she answered coolly, leaning against the glass-and-steel bookshelf in the corner. In the past, if a college guy offered her a drink at a party, she would've had to carefully consider all of the ramifications of accepting. But now that she was practically engaged, she felt immune to the flirtations of those around her—college boys or otherwise.

"I'm Ellis." Brad Pitt held his hand out politely. He was sort of like an anti-Easy, which made her miss Easy even more.

"Callie." She tossed her head slightly, her shoulder-length blond hair bobbing in its loose ponytail. "How do you know Yvonne?" Meaning, how does a hot guy know Yvonne Stidder? She casually ran her finger across the thick architectural books lining the sleek bookshelves.

"I went to prep school with Jeremy. Her brother." He pointed out onto the roof deck, but it was momentarily empty.

"I'm home from Princeton." He smiled into his martini before taking a drink.

"Princeton," Callie repeated, impressed. She'd always thought of Princeton as one of those boring ultra-competitive schools where nerds holed up in the library for weeks at a time studying, but now she imagined an ivy-covered campus filled with guys who looked like Brad Pitt. "Do you like it there?"

Ellis nodded, leaning against the back of a bright red chair that looked like it came from *The Jetsons*. "I miss the city, though. I've lived here all my life." He ran his hand through his blond hair. "So, what are you doing while you're here?"

"I'm actually meeting up with my boyfriend." She tossed out the word *boyfriend* effortlessly, watching Ellis's face for a reaction. "We haven't seen each other in a while."

"I know how hard that is," Ellis confided, his light green eyes sympathetic. "My girlfriend lives in Belgium."

"Wow, that's far." Callie stared out at the dark again, immediately conjuring up a French-speaking, big-lipped Angelina Jolie–like girlfriend for him. She wondered how she would feel knowing Easy was on another *continent*. She took another sip of her drink, not realizing she'd sucked half of it down already. Jenny, sitting on the couch with Kara, caught her eye. Callie gave her a look that said she was just talking, that nothing was going on. He had a girlfriend, she thought, almost gleefully. It was extra-okay to just-talk to him.

"It's not that bad. It's kind of like flying from here to California," Ellis said. "I just don't get to go that often, is all. She comes over sometimes, but her family is over there—her father's a diplomat—so it's not as easy for her." He looked forlorn and Callie could feel his pain.

"What's her name?" Callie asked, feigning interest in an oversize book on modern Brazilian architecture.

"Sybil," Ellis answered wistfully. It looked for a moment like he might drift off into a reverie, then he took another sip from his martini. "What about you? What's your guy's story?"

"Easy goes to school in West Virginia . . . but he's sneaking away for the weekend." Saying it out loud made her shiver—she hadn't thought about how after their romantic weekend Easy would be forced to go back to military school. Would he be in trouble? Where do you go if you get kicked out of military school? Prison? "He gave me this." She flashed him her promise ring.

"That's impressive." Ellis scratched his neck, and Callie caught sight of a thin platinum chain around his neck. "To find someone like that. Especially while still in high school." Callie searched his face for traces of condescension—it sounded like something Tinsley would say—but found none. She read in Ellis's face that he, too, had found the person he wanted to spend the rest of his life with. "Your boyfriend is a lucky guy," he added. "Hope he knows it."

"Me too," Callie giggled. Just one more night and she'd be with Easy again. "Here's to . . . uh . . . long-distance love." She raised her glass, and Ellis touched his to hers.

"Amen," he said. "Except your glass is empty. I'll get you a refill."

* * *

From across the room, Jenny eyed Callie and one of Jeremy Stidder's cute college friends huddled in the corner. "Is he a friend of yours?" she asked Casey, the cute college boy who was huddled next to *her*. He'd sat down on the black leather couch with her and Kara and joined their discussion about where to find the best diner food in the city. When Rifat Jones had called Kara away to play air hockey in the game room, Casey had slid a few inches closer to Jenny.

"That's Ellis." Casey followed Jenny's eyes across the room, a curl of dark hair falling down over his forehead. "We've hung out some. He's cool. He's got a girlfriend."

"And what about you?" Jenny turned her attention back to their flirtation. Casey had initiated it, telling her how much she looked like a movie star whose name he couldn't remember. He was totally cute—in a vintage-looking Thundercats T-shirt and a pair of black dress pants, he looked like some kind of alt-rocker on a night off.

"No girlfriend," he said, crossing his heart. "Can you believe it?"

"Barely." Jenny laughed, leaning her head back against the couch and staring at the ceiling. People swirled around them, but it felt like they were all alone in their own world.

He leaned against the flat gray pillow in the corner of the couch, and it was all Jenny could do to keep from tackling him, feeling his broad chest against her cheek. Was she drunk already? "So, how do you know Yvonne, anyway?" he asked, his gray-brown eyes flashing.

Jenny bit her lip, reluctant to break the spell of their flirtation by saying she was in high school. Would he be freaked out? "Waverly," she finally answered.

"No shit." He grinned. "I go to Union. It's, like, half an hour from you."

"That's so cool." A vision of her striding confidently across the Union College campus on weekend visits, waving hello to Casey's friends, hearing whispers of *That's Casey's girlfriend*, filled her imagination. She could see herself arriving at wild frat parties, holding hands with him.

"Yeah, totally cool," Casey agreed, scratching his knee. "Union's a great place."

Jenny suddenly realized that she was still wearing her ugly lumpy oatmeal sweater—her train wear—and not a streak of makeup. She probably looked like a lumpy batch of oatmeal herself. "Hey, save my seat," she said, coyly, setting her empty cosmo on the glass-topped coffee table. "I've got to take my sweater off—it's really warm in here." She dashed off in the direction of her suitcase to retrieve something cuter and her makeup bag. She slipped into a guest room just as Tinsley exited, a determined look on her face.

"I've got to change," Jenny whispered, tugging off her sweater. "I didn't realize I looked like such a bum."

"You don't look too bad." Tinsley tilted her head to the side, her hair sweeping over her shoulders. "But I've seen you look better."

Tinsley left Jenny behind and crept down the hallway, looking around for any sign of the poisonous Sleigh Monroe-Hill, who would probably start a catfight right in the middle of the party, screaming at Tinsley for getting her kicked out of school. Whatever. It wasn't like Tinsley had been the one to dump *her* entire lingerie drawer out on the front lawn. (She was pretty sure Heath Ferro had snatched her favorite Agent Provocateur bikini briefs from the bushes, but he still denied it.)

She spotted Callie and a gorgeous guy chatting each other up by the glass doors that looked out onto the patio. Interesting. Apparently, she had abandoned her wedding dress fantasy. At least Yvonne's party wasn't a total nerdfest. Tinsley's nerves felt alive, and she sensed that something very interesting could happen. As she entered the kitchen, she was wholly disappointed to see a pack of complete dorks—probably from Yvonne's jazz band—holding court in the mahogany and stainless steel room. The skinny, awkward kids sipped Bacardi wine coolers.

Tinsley placed a hand on her hip. "Anyone know where the liquor is hiding?"

She peeked into a cupboard but saw only boxes of Froot Loops.

"I can make you a cosmo, Tinsley." A short blond guy whose head only came up to Tinsley's chin immediately jumped forward, grabbing a silver shaker and a martini glass. She paused for a second, wondering if she knew this loser. And then it clicked. It was Julian's roommate, Kevin.

"I don't drink pink things," she replied, taking the martini glass out of his hand and grabbing the bottle of Absolut. "But thank you."

She didn't know what made her look up at that moment

into the dining room, but she did. Her eyes landed on a guy standing by himself, staring at an enormous red and orange Jackson Pollock–y painting, deep in thought. Julian. Julian was here. She actually felt her heart shiver, if that was possible. She could still hear Julian's last words to her, when she'd asked why she hadn't seen him at the Waverly Halloween party: *Even if I had gone, I wouldn't have wanted to hang out with you.* It was far from the meanest thing anyone had ever said to her, but coming from Julian, who was the coolest guy she'd ever met, it had stung more than anything else.

Abruptly, Tinsley stepped away, leaning back against the kitchen counter. Kevin, who was completely blitzed, offered to make her a martini, but instead of answering, she spun on her heel and stalked out of the room. Martini glass and bottle of vodka in hand, she returned to the guest bedroom and collapsed on the bed.

It wasn't Halloween anymore, but everyone from her past was coming back to haunt her.

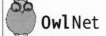

EmilyJenkins: OMG, you won't believe who's at Yvonne
Stidder's party.

BennyCunningham: Who? A bunch o' losers? Ha!

EmilyJenkins: Hell, no. EVERY Owl in NYC is here—including
Callie, Jenny, and Tinsley . . . and Sleigh
Monroe-Hill!

BennyCunningham: That wench told me freshman year that she
knew a dermatologist who could do wonders
for my face—in front of Tom Pham, who I was
totally trying to get with!

EmilyJenkins: You did have some serious acne that year. . . .

BennyCunningham: Not so! It was an allergy to my field hockey
uniform. Doesn't excuse her from being a
BITCH!

EmilyJenkins: I think she has some kind of folk record out. . . .

BennyCunningham: More like a HO record. I'd like to see her and
T.C. duke it out!

A SMART OWL KNOWS THAT THE BEST ADVICE

COMES FROM UNEXPECTED SOURCES.

Jenny dabbed her Cargo PlantLove lipstick in Cherry Bliss carefully across her lips, making them look soft and sweet and extra-kissable. She'd spent an hour talking to Casey already, and wanted to spend the next hour talking to him too—and hopefully, he'd be thinking about kissing her. Would she let him? The answer was . . . she didn't know. She knew she *shouldn't*—she'd met him about an hour ago—but there was a whole list of things that she shouldn't do, and where was the fun in that? Having pulled off her heavy sweater to reveal her black, sheer gauze Free People top with the flutter sleeves, she felt much more in the mood for fun.

The bathroom door flew open, sending Jenny crashing toward the mirror, her left hand almost jabbing the mascara wand directly into her eye.

"What—" Jenny started, surprised to see Tinsley in the doorway.

"Sorry, I thought no one was in here," Tinsley mumbled, stepping backwards. "It's okay," Jenny insisted. "You can come in."

"Thanks." Tinsley closed the door behind her, martini glass in hand.

"So." Jenny felt the need to say something, as she and Tinsley weren't exactly close enough to hang out in a strange bathroom in perfect silence. "I just met the perfect guy." She brought her lips together to smooth out the gloss, the taste of cherry teasing the tip of her tongue.

"Me too," Tinsley answered softly, looking at herself in the mirror sternly. Jenny noticed with interest that it wasn't a *Do I look hot?* look—Tinsley always looked hot, but especially tonight in her black wrap dress and dangling leaf-shaped earrings—but more like a *Where am I?* look.

A shiver ran through Jenny. She didn't mean she'd met Casey too, did she? "Who?" she asked, a little afraid of the answer.

Tinsley put her hands on her hips and cast her gaze toward the floor, looking like she was about to throw up. Jenny braced for the worst—that Casey was an old boyfriend and they were taking off to spend Thanksgiving in some downtown penthouse surrounded by supermodels and movie stars, leaving Jenny to crawl back to her father and the Hare Krishnas. "Julian."

"What?" Jenny inadvertently dropped her mascara wand, and it clattered against the clear glass sink bowl, leaving black smudges in its wake. Was Julian McCafferty *here*? It didn't seem that long ago that Jenny was convinced she was in love with the cute, super-tall freshman—but once she'd found out that he'd been hooking up with Tinsley Carmichael just a few days before *they* got together, that had been the end of things.

Jenny could see Tinsley's hands were shaking. "I told you I'd been in love before."

"I thought you were talking about that guy in Africa, or some European prince." Julian? He was so . . . normal. "Or a rock star."

Tinsley laughed, color starting to come back into her cheeks. "Nope, just a freshman." Jenny's mind reeled—if Tinsley had really been in love with Julian, no wonder she'd gone on a rampage against Jenny after finding out that they were together. Not that it made trying to pin the blame on her for starting the barn fire any more acceptable—but maybe a little more understandable. Tinsley pulled open a drawer in the vanity and absently began sifting through it. "I've never felt the way he makes me feel before. He's so open and honest. With, like, no ulterior motives, you know?" Tinsley's eyes widened, as if suddenly remembering she was talking to someone who had hooked up with him too. "I mean, not that you would know— er, well, I guess you might, but that's not what I meant—"

"I know." Jenny peered into the open drawer. She and Tinsley spotted the box of Trojans—extra-large, Ultra Pleasure.

"Ew, that is so gross." Tinsley slammed the drawer shut. "Is this, like, Mr. and Mrs. Stidder's bathroom? Who the hell leaves condoms for guests?"

"Maybe they're just considerate." Jenny's giggles quickly turned into hiccups, and Tinsley gave her a quick slap on the back to make her stop. A moment passed, and Jenny felt much more comfortable with the glamorous older girl than she ever had before. "You know, there really wasn't anything between me and Julian."

Was that true? It certainly hadn't felt like it at the time—but over a month had passed since Jenny last spoke to him, and she hadn't exactly been pining over him all this time. In her wildest dreams she wouldn't have thought Tinsley and Julian had more than a few random hookups between them, but the look on Tinsley's face made it clear that she had fallen hard.

"I can't get him off my mind," Tinsley admitted, leaning over the sink and splashing cold water on her face.

Jenny sat down on the closed toilet seat. Julian and Tinsley? She waited for the familiar pang of jealousy she'd experienced moments earlier when she thought Tinsley had lassoed Casey out from under her, but there was nothing. And she really thought she'd been in love with Julian. She could remember a night not so long ago when she'd stared out her dorm room window at the stars, wondering if Julian was somehow looking at the same thing.

But then she remembered the exact same scenario—that new-love feeling—except with Drew . . . and she shuddered.

Staring fixedly at the small tray of aromatic candles perched on the floor next to the claw-foot tub, she remembered thinking about Easy in the exact same way. She'd only been at Waverly since September—and she'd already been in love three times.

"I wish I were more like you." Tinsley sighed, sinking down on the edge of the tub, pressing her black-stockinged knees together.

"What?" Jenny squealed. Tinsley Carmichael, the most glamorous person ever to set her Manolos onto Waverly's leafy campus, wished she were like Jenny Humphrey, who had just spent an hour flirting with a guy while wearing a giant, butt-ugly sweater? "In what way?"

"I don't know." Tinsley sighed, tracing her fingers across the brass fixtures of the tub. "I mean, this is the only time I've ever felt this way, but I never even let Julian have any idea. I was just kind of my regular, bossy self." She eyed Jenny again, her violet eyes beautiful and sad. "I can see why he liked you better."

"Maybe he just wanted to get to know you," Jenny suggested, twirling the bangle bracelet on her wrist. "And you wouldn't let him."

Tinsley nodded and picked up a bottle of L'Occitane Lavender bubble bath. She twisted off the top, took a sniff, and set it back down. "I mean, I see the way people react to you. You're so easy to get along with."

"It's not a trick." Jenny stood up, brushing off her dark J Brand jeans with the crooked hems—she'd had to cut about a foot off the bottom and stitch them up herself. "I just like meeting people."

"I don't." Tinsley wrinkled her nose. "It upsets my balance. I hate having to constantly reconfigure everyone, who fits where and all that."

"Is that why you're so cold to people when you first meet them?" Jenny asked her reflection. She wouldn't have dared risk the question earlier, especially on the train, when Tinsley had been in her perpetually sour mood.

Tinsley pursed her lips together. "I guess so."

A loud knock startled them both and Tinsley strode over and pulled open the door. "What?" she demanded of the poor girl quavering there. "There are other bathrooms, you know. This one's full." Tinsley slammed the door closed again before the girl could get a word out.

"Well, if you want to get Julian back, you're going to have to quit the ice queen business," Jenny said abruptly. She realized it sounded a little harsh, and that Tinsley hadn't actually asked for her advice, so she added, "In my opinion."

"I don't know what you mean," Tinsley said coldly, crossing her arms.

Jenny chanced it, pushing on. "That," she said, pointing in the mirror. "You just got defensive. Don't do that. It's okay to risk rejection. You know what my brother says? 'A pretty girl can't tell you no if you don't ask her out.' I always think of that when I worry about failing."

"I'm sure it's too late now." Tinsley suppressed a smirk. "Julian would never like me again, after what I did to you." She sucked in her cheeks.

Jenny turned to face her. "All I'm saying is, it's clear that you're really in love with Julian," she continued, "and you need to be open with him. Don't try to outmaneuver him into liking you again, because it won't work. Just . . . you know . . . apologize to him for everything and tell him how you feel. If he won't hear it, well, it's his loss." She stuffed her tube of lip gloss back into her purse.

Tinsley smiled. "Thanks," she said softly. "Maybe I will."

"Good." Jenny opened the door, but Tinsley braced against it, shutting it again, to a chorus of groans on the other side.

"One word of advice for you, then, since we're in share mode." Tinsley playfully wagged a finger at Jenny, but her eyes were serious. "Don't start thinking about prom with this guy you just met. You really do need to slow down and just have fun."

Jenny stared at her lips in the mirror. Okay, so she kind of had been planning her first trip to Union already. "Does that mean I can't kiss him?"

"Since when did I become a nun?" Tinsley rolled her eyes. "Of course you can kiss him. Just don't start, you know, picking out your ring yet."

"Okay, that's fair," Jenny agreed.

"Break a few hearts yourself before letting yours get broken again, 'kay?"

Jenny took one last glance at herself in the mirror. Next to Tinsley, she looked . . . well, not as bad as she'd thought.

Tinsley caught her glance in the mirror. "We've both got our work cut out for us." She gave her a slight push toward the door, and Jenny opened it. A crowd of girls dying to pee broke into applause.

Kara pulled Jenny to the side as Tinsley strode out. "I saw her go in there—I thought maybe she was strangling you!" She wore a questioning look. "What were you guys doing?"

Jenny just smiled. "You wouldn't believe me if I told you."

A WAVERLY OWL IS NICE TO HER ENEMIES—
PARTICULARLY WHEN A CUTE BOY IS WATCHING.

Tinsley pushed through the intimate crowd, making her way back to the kitchen. The penthouse smelled rank with sour cigarette smoke and too much cologne and perfume in too small a space. Her throat was dry from her talk with Jenny, and so was her martini glass.

As if fate were tempting her to test out Jenny's advice, the only person in the kitchen was the one she most—and least—wanted to see. Julian stood in front of the refrigerator, staring at the closed door. Tinsley froze in her tracks. He looked gorgeous in a green and gray striped cardigan over a white T-shirt, black Levi's, and his faded black Chuck Taylors. Her stomach fluttered.

She tried to peer over his shoulder to see what had captured his attention, wondering if there was a funny family photo of Yvonne wearing something stupid, or an overly clever refrigerator magnet with a pithy saying.

"Produce," a voice said, and it took a moment or two for Tinsley to realize it wasn't Julian but the refrigerator. Julian opened and closed the fridge door. "Beer," the same electronic voice said.

"Hey," Tinsley said softly, not wanting to startle him.

Julian jumped anyway, turning to look at her. The surprise in his buttery brown eyes made her smile involuntarily. "Hey." He ran his hand through his shaggy brown-blond hair, which he'd cut. It was no longer as sun-bleached, either, and it made him look older. In a good way. "What are you doing here?"

She searched his voice for any hint of annoyance or anger, but couldn't discern any. "My parents are having their floors done," she said by way of explanation, though she could tell the answer only confused him. So she launched into the whole saga, breathlessly relating how Jenny's father was in a cult and how all the hotels were full and so they'd ended up at Yvonne's.

Julian smiled. The tiny dimple to the left of his mouth was like an old friend to Tinsley. An old friend she wanted to lick. "It's like that movie *After Hours*."

"I don't know that one." She loved that Julian was a film buff like her, but she also hated it when she didn't get a film reference. In fact, Tinsley felt the same way about Julian's film knowledge as she did about him: She kind of hated it, because he was a freshman and shouldn't know more than her, and she kind of loved it. "What are *you* doing here?" she asked, leaning against the granite countertop and trying not to look like she was trying to look sexy—which she was. "I mean, besides talking to a refrigerator."

Julian kind of smiled. She wondered if he just felt awkward, or if he maybe felt kind of bad about the last thing he'd said to her. Not that it wasn't true or that she didn't deserve it—but she could see him feeling bad anyway, and a surge of hope dashed through her veins. "Seattle's too far to go home for Thanksgiving, and I'm a vegetarian anyway, so it's kind of hard to look forward to a long flight just for some—"

"Tofurkey?" Tinsley suggested, grabbing a few cashews from the bowl of mixed nuts on the table. "I didn't know you were a vegetarian."

Julian stared straight at her, and Tinsley felt a chill run down her spine all the way to her toes. "There are a lot of things you don't know about me." Her heart sank, and she had a feeling he was about to leave.

"Milk," the refrigerator said abruptly, causing them both to laugh.

"I think it's on the fritz." Julian jammed a thumb in the air and stepped away from the refrigerator in one smooth move. "I guess it's some kind of high-tech grocery alert system."

Neither of them said anything for a beat, the noise from the living room wafting through. Someone screamed the lyrics of a Radiohead song at the top of their lungs, but was quickly drowned out by a chorus of "Shut up!" Julian stared at the floor, toeing the tile with his sneakers. Tinsley felt a tingle as she remembered Jenny's words.

"Listen, Julian." She gulped, staring down at the pen mark

on the white plastic toe of his shoe. She hated it when people started sentences by saying, *Listen.* "I'm sorry." The words came out stubbornly, but relief washed over her the minute she'd said them.

She could feel Julian's eyes on her, and she wished she had a drink or a cigarette or some other prop to hide her nerves. "What for?"

"Everything." She turned away from him slightly, grabbing the bottle of vodka and pouring a splash into her empty martini glass on the counter. "I'm sorry for the way I treated you, for acting so cool toward you when we were, you know . . ." She let her voice trail sexily—she couldn't help it. Christ, why was it so hard to be sincere? To shut off the act? Then she realized she *was* sincere. And once she'd opened the floodgates of apology, she couldn't hold back. "I'm sorry for what happened with Jenny, too. We talked it over and we're . . . It's fine now."

"Yeah?"

"Yeah." Tinsley nodded slowly, staring at a dish of hummus and carrots. "She's like a thousand times nicer than me. If I were her, I probably never would have forgiven me."

"That's probably true."

Tinsley had the feeling that he was being a hardass to test her, to see if she'd bristle and throw some snide comment at him. But she didn't feel that way at all, even if she was embarrassed to be so humbled in stupid Yvonne Stidder's kitchen. "But I wanted to say I'm sorry to *you* because I know you probably think I'm the most evil person in the world, but I'm really not." Her voice trembled a little, unintentionally.

"I don't think you're the most evil person in the world." Julian grabbed a Heineken from the fridge and cracked it open. Tinsley wondered if she'd imagined the emphasis on the word *most*. But it was too late to turn back now.

"I was just jealous." She lowered her eyes and peeked up at him through her long, thick lashes. It was a move she'd used many times to look humble when she wasn't feeling humble at all, but now it was just too hard to look straight at Julian. It was like he was the sun or something and she had to shield her eyes. "And I completely regret it now. I can't even think about it without being disgusted by how I behaved. I'm really not a bad person." She reined in her heavy breathing, stifling the sob that she could feel developing in her chest. "I'm nicer than you think I am."

Julian stared at her, confused. He took his hands out of his pockets, and then sank them back in again. She'd broken through his cool reserve, she could tell.

"I'm not sure if I believe you," he said finally, "but it would be nice if it were true."

"Give me a chance to prove it," Tinsley pleaded. She'd come too far to turn back, and she knew she wouldn't be denied. "Maybe we can spend some time together."

Julian smiled and shrugged. "Okay," he said simply. "I think I'd like that."

"Hey, you coming, Jules?" An unwelcomely familiar voice spoke up from the doorway, and Tinsley didn't even have

to raise her eyes to know it was Sleigh Monroe-Hill. *Jules?*
"I've got my YouTube video all loaded, as promised. You
said you—" She stopped short when she saw Tinsley, her
wide blue eyes flying open. "Oh my God, is that *Tinsley Carmichael?*"

Her voice was coated in sugar and it was all Tinsley could
do not to gag. But there was no way she was going to let Sleigh
ruin her fresh start with Julian. Tinsley opened her mouth to
say something polite yet noncommittal (after all, the last time
Tinsley had seen her, Sleigh's dad was writing a fat check to
Tinsley for her laptop and all the other shit she'd ruined), but
before she could, Sleigh enveloped her in a massive bear hug.
"God, it's been too long, T.C." Tinsley hugged her back limply.
Since when was Sleigh friendly? Or even nice? "You look *glamorous,* as usual!"

With that little comment, Tinsley knew nothing had
changed. Sleigh said "glamorous" as if it was an insult—one
that only girls could hear. "Yeah, it's been a while." Tinsley
backed away from Sleigh, taking in her hippie lavender tank
top (um, it was snowing out) and her sun-bleached hair (had
she just been to the Caribbean?). Was she actually not wearing
a bra? But Tinsley felt Julian's eyes on her, so she quickly said,
"You look great, too, Sleigh."

Sleigh's blue eyes flickered briefly before she grabbed Julian's
hand. "C'mon, everyone is waiting."

"Okay, I'm coming." Julian gave Tinsley one last look
before they both disappeared into the front room, leaving her

alone in the suddenly empty kitchen. She was mildly curious about the video, but a more pressing question squeezed itself to the front of her brain: *How in the hell did Sleigh even know Julian?*

"Butter," the fridge said, as if that answered her question.

14

A WAVERLY OWL KNOWS THAT YOU'RE NEVER TOO
OLD FOR A SLEEPOVER.

Jenny leaned back against the sleek black bookcase, watching the snow come down outside the library window. It had a clear view of the rooftop deck, and a few brave souls loitered in the hot tub there, drunkenly enjoying the winter wonderland spreading across the rooftops along Park Avenue. The snow had picked up in intensity over the last few hours, but Jenny hardly noticed. She hardly noticed anything at all besides Casey—time sailed by as she chatted with him about everything from their favorite movies to bands they loved to places Casey had traveled.

"Phuket is probably the most beautiful place I've visited," he said, tracing a finger across the antique globe in its dark wooden stand. "You should go when you get a chance." Jenny wouldn't mind going—with Casey. But then she remembered Tinsley's admonition to keep things light, and to have fun. And a trip to Thailand probably violated that rule—although she imagined it would certainly count as having fun.

"Look." Emily Jenkins waved toward the window, and a dozen drunken Owls huddled around her, looking down at the street below. Jenny shook her head to clear her thoughts—she hadn't even noticed that there was anyone else in the room—and rushed to the window with Casey. A bus had stalled out in the middle of the snow-packed intersection of Eightieth and Park Avenue. A cacophony of horns sounded, and moments later the street was snarled with traffic, a layer of snow quickly accumulating on all the cars. The entire scene looked miniature, like a snow globe someone had just shaken.

Yvonne climbed up onto the sleek mahogany executive's desk in the corner. She wavered, barely able to stand from drinking her weight in rum and Diet Cokes. "Anyone who needs a place to crash can camp out here!" she shrieked happily. Yvonne had been circling around the party all night, drunk not just from the booze, but giddy about how well her party had turned out. "It'll be like a giant slumber party—my parents are in London until Monday, so you guys're all invited to Thanksgiving!" Her speech was slurred, and Jenny worried she might topple over onto the hardwood floor. "Pizza on me. It'll be the best!"

"Wow, she's plowed," Casey whispered, leaning closer to Jenny.

Jenny nodded, staring into his dark brown eyes. There was a ring of gray around his pupil, something Jenny had never seen before. He was taller than Jenny—practically everybody past the age of ten was—but he wasn't as toweringly tall as most of the boys Jenny fell for, and it was nice to not have to arch her neck just to look up at him.

Or kiss him, she thought, her pulse starting to race.

"Are you staying?" Casey asked, as if reading her mind. He set his empty plastic cup next to the globe on the end table.

"Are you?" she asked casually. She flipped her hair to show that she could stay or she could go, though in reality she had nowhere to go. Back to her dad's? Even if she wanted to, it would've been a nightmare to get across the snow-bound city.

"Yeah," he answered, and Jenny swore his eyes rested for a split second on her lips.

A spike of electricity shot up Jenny's spine. "Me too." She smiled. "All the hotels are booked anyway," she added, surprised at how cosmopolitan she sounded.

"Great." Casey smiled.

The lights dimmed as the evening moved past midnight. The flat screen above the fireplace showed *Mean Girls* on mute while people around it played cards and drunkenly made up their own lines from the movie. The snow slowed down and the hot tub reopened for business. A wet trail of slush ran from the roof deck into the living room, and everyone yelled when the door opened and a cold blast of air shot through the apartment. Julian stood near the large corner fireplace, turning over the logs with a poker, as a blond girl Jenny didn't recognize sat on a pillow at his feet, cross-legged, as if she were meditating or in some yoga class. Jenny looked around for Tinsley, wondering if she'd managed to talk to him yet, but only spotted Callie, sitting in an ultramodern teardrop-shaped red chair, chatting intensely with the boy next to her.

The night collapsed into murmurs as everyone claimed beds or carved out a spot in the front room with the sleeping bags and blankets and pillows someone had unearthed from a hall closet. Jenny couldn't remember who had pulled the couch out, or how she ended up lounging on it next to Casey, but she liked it.

"You're shivering." He reached into the foggy darkness and pulled up the warm down blanket. He draped the comforter over her and tucked it in under her chin, his hands patting her body tentatively.

"Thanks." His face was so close she could kiss it, and Casey leaned in as if he might beat her to it, but instead he just pushed a thick curl behind her ear, his fingers lingering slightly.

"Sweet dreams," he whispered, tucking a pillow under his head, and as Jenny drifted off to sleep, she realized she was already having them.

A WAVERLY OWL IS OPEN TO NEW EXPERIENCES.

The steps to Mr. Dunderdorf's white clapboard house at the north edge of campus were covered in a thick layer of snow, and Heath clambered up them eagerly. Brandon hung back, wondering what the fuck they were doing awake at this hour, on Thanksgiving morning, when they were supposed to be on vacation. He almost wished that he was at home, tucked into his own bed, letting the "ocean wave" setting of his Bose sound machine block out the noises of two rambunctious toddlers as they watched *Thomas the Tank Engine* and turned the living room into a war zone. Nowhere was safe anymore, apparently. But he knew the second Heath jumped out of bed at 5 a.m., before the sun even broke the horizon, that it was going to be a long, long day. Brandon had tried to roll over, burying his head under his down pillow, but Heath wouldn't let up. "The Dunderdorf twins are waiting for us," he just kept chanting over and over before Brandon relented, falling asleep in the shower for a minute until the hot water ran cold.

Now, Heath flashed Brandon a double thumbs-up and rapped on the weather-beaten Dunderdorf front door. The hot smell of the oven greeted them when the door flew open. "Come in," Mr. Dunderdorf thundered, his voice impossibly deep for a frail-looking man.

"Is he wearing *lederhosen*?" Brandon whispered to Heath as Dunderdorf waved them through the solid oak doorway and into the living room, which was an alpine nightmare of paneled walls and shelves of dusty knickknacks. He stared at Dunderdorf's dark green leather pants, which came to his knees, and under which he had some kind of wooly tights.

"Lederhosen *are* the traditional Bavarian men's clothing," Heath hissed back. "Don't be such a hater."

Brandon's eyes adjusted to the half-light, taking in the carvings of elves and gnomes that screamed out from everywhere. One particular carving—of a giant elf with a menacing pig face—really freaked Brandon out. A table in the corner housed an entire ceramic village, each house painted a different primary color, all the roofs lacquered with a coat of fake snow. A strand of Christmas lights snaked through the village, blinking red and green and yellow and pink and blue every thirty seconds.

A chime sounded, and before Brandon could steady himself, the cuckoo clock on the wall struck eight. A tiny yodeler—in lederhosen—shot out on a plank, his demonic little face worn from years of exposure.

"Dude, that guy in the clock doesn't have a face," Heath noted.

"I saw it." Brandon suddenly felt like he was caught in some kind of cross-cultural time warp. He had to look down at his faded True Religion jeans and familiar Burberry down-filled vest to remind himself he wasn't on another planet.

"Frau Dunderdorf and I are in the middle of Dutch Blitz." Mr. Dunderdorf stuck his thumbs under the suspenders of his short-pants and pulled them from his chest. "Do you know how to play?"

Brandon was about to say no—who played cards at this hour?—when Heath jumped in. "No, sir, but we'd love to learn."

Patting Heath on the back, Dunderdorf led them through the front room and into the stifling kitchen, where a short, portly woman who bore a striking resemblance to Mr. Dunderdorf sat behind a metal table strewn with cards neither of them recognized. "This is Mrs. Dunderdorf."

Heath and Brandon nodded hello. *How did these two produce a pair of knockout twins?* Brandon thought. He wanted to ask Heath if he'd actually seen these legendary twins, but he could tell Heath was as freaked out as he was.

"Wow, those cards are funky." Heath's voice almost squeaked with panic.

"Ah . . ." Mr. Dunderdorf waved him off. "It's easy. Sit down."

They cautiously took their seats around the table and Brandon's attention wandered as Mr. Dunderdorf explained about the four decks—Pump, Buggy, Plow, and Bucket—and how every deck had ten each of red, blue, green, and yellow cards.

Brandon stared at the little Dutchman who appeared in each of the cards' four corners, wondering if he'd somehow stepped into the Twilight Zone. At least he wasn't thinking about Sage, wondering what she was doing . . . although, now that he thought about it, what *was* she doing? And what, for that matter, was *he* doing?

"What's the matter?" Mrs. Dunderdorf asked, her kindly Mrs. Claus blue eyes focused on Brandon's face.

"Nothing," Brandon assured her. "Just, uh, looking forward to some . . ." He trailed off, searching his brain for the word for *German sausage.* "*Deutsche Wurst.*"

Mrs. Dunderdorf grinned at him, revealing a gap between her front teeth large enough to stick a pencil through. Mr. Dunderdorf commenced the first round of Dutch Blitz, which turned out to be a lot like Uno. After about twenty minutes of intense card play, Mrs. Dunderdorf brought over the coffee pot and filled their mugs. Brandon gave Heath a sharp kick in the shin, but Heath just gave him a helpless *I know, dude, but what do you want me to do* look.

Mr. Dunderdorf excused himself to use the *Raum des Kleinen Jungen*—Brandon thought that meant "little boy's room," but it had been a few years since he'd been in German class. Once he was out of earshot, Heath leaned forward and asked Mrs. Dunderdorf, "So, uh, are your daughters still asleep?" The question sounded innocent enough, but Brandon winced when it left Heath's lips.

Mrs. Dunderdorf shook her head and Brandon braced for the bad news that either they weren't coming or they'd never even existed. Maybe some evil senior had started the rumor, know-ing that some horny soul would try to exploit it.

"Their plane was delayed," Mrs. Dunderdorf answered, shuffling the cards. "We will pick them up later."

What? Heath refused to look at Brandon, pretending to con-centrate on his cards instead. They'd dragged their asses over here practically at the crack of dawn—for nothing! At least they were coming, though.

"Now it is time to get the turkey," Mr. Dunderdorf announced, returning to the kitchen and clapping his hands together. His face looked positively gleeful. "Follow me."

Brandon and Heath pushed away from the table and got to their feet, eager at the chance to avoid another round of Dutch Blitz. Maybe a trip in to Rhinecliff's Stop & Shop would give them an opportunity to escape—or, Brandon reasoned to him-self, at least to "remember" an "important project" he needed to work on. They could come back later—or tomorrow—to catch a glimpse of the twins.

"Thank you for the delicious coffee, Mrs. Dunderdorf." Heath smiled ingratiatingly, never willing to give up. "It hit the spot."

Mr. Dunderdorf led them outside, the morning chill hanging in the air, but rather than heading for the Volkswagen parked in the driveway, he took them around the side of the house. Brandon froze in his tracks when he heard what he hoped he hadn't.

Mr. Dunderdorf opened the gate into the small backyard. A large turkey paced the length of the lawn, stopping and staring at them before skittering away. "C'mon, boys, it's just a little bird." He chuckled to himself.

"Oh, hell no." Brandon shook his head and leaned back against the gate, trying to signal to Heath that now was the time to run. This was it. No twins, just a live turkey and a house that smelled like his Grandma Ginny's.

"Dude," Heath exhaled, his face ashen. "This is bad."

Mr. Dunderdorf, oblivious to their distress, motioned to the cage in the corner. "We need to get him back inside, boys," he said. "You have to chase him, or he won't move. You can't just walk up to him." The old man took off running at the turkey, who fluttered his wings and scampered in the opposite direction of the open cage.

"I'm not doing this," Brandon declared, running his hand through his short, golden-brown hair.

"Dude, it'll be worth it." Heath planted both his hands on Brandon's shoulders. "Do you have any idea how delicious these twins are? Do you have any idea how legendary we'll be come Monday morning? Sage will probably hear about it and be all like, 'Oh, what did I doooo?'" Heath used his high-pitched girl voice to imitate Sage.

It worked. Brandon loved the idea of Sage finding out he'd gotten together with a hot German chick just days after she'd tried to break his heart. It was enough to send him racing around the yard, chasing the giant, stupid bird. Brandon's heart beat wildly in his chest as they tried to maneuver the turkey toward the cage—but it always veered away from the open door at the last minute, circling the yard as it called loudly. Breathless, he stopped, his hands on his knees, watching as Mr. Dunderdorf and Heath brought the cage to the turkey, cornering it in the yard until it had no choice but to waddle inside.

"Aha!" Mr. Dunderdorf exclaimed as he locked the cage door. "Good work, Mr. Ferro." He picked up an ax. "Now, for the messy part."

An hour later, after washing up, when Heath and Brandon were still too traumatized to speak, Mr. Dunderdorf announced that it was the perfect time for a sauna.

"A sauna?" Brandon choked out, too weak to resist as Mr. Dunderdorf led him and Heath down the basement stairs. The smell of wet wood filled Brandon's nostrils, and the darkness was suddenly illuminated to reveal a full sauna behind a glass door, the wooden benches lit under the red lights. Mr. Dunderdorf adjusted the dial on the outside of the door and began to disrobe.

"Leave your clothes outside," Mr. Dunderdorf instructed. "Use the hooks." He pointed to a series of hooks on the wall.

Brandon watched to see if Heath's first instinct was the same as his own—to bolt—but Heath turned his back on Mr. Dunderdorf and started to take his clothes off. Mr. Dunderdorf took a fresh towel out of the wicker basket by the door and strode into the sauna, the glass door clicking behind him.

"No way," Brandon said.

"Trust me, dude," Heath said, standing in his boxers. "It's totally going to be worth it. You've come this far."

Brandon nodded. Heath was right. He just needed the Dunderdorf twins to arrive, and fast, so that Sage could hear about it, get insanely jealous, and beg him to take her back.

He stripped down to his navy and yellow striped Ralph Lauren boxers, threw his clothes in a pile next to Heath's, and grabbed a towel.

16

A WAVERLY OWL LETS HER TRUE COLORS SHINE THROUGH.

Strains of classical music played through the recessed speakers of the Messerschmidts' built-in surround-sound system on Thursday morning. Brett stared miserably down at the caviar torte with champagne onions, a dish she'd never heard of, let alone seen served in her house. She squinted across the polished oak dining room table at Bree, whom she held personally responsible for the monstrosity. When she'd promised her mother to behave at Thanksgiving brunch with the Coopers, Brett had imagined she'd be aided in this endeavor by quietly munching away on her mother's airy French toast, and not something concocted out of gelatinous fish eggs. She felt her throat constrict as she forked a piece of the torte, wriggling it free and pushing it around her plate, the immaculate china shiny as a mirror.

But Brianna, in a maidenly blue Ann Taylor dress covered

in a tiny rose print, refused to acknowledge her, as she'd done since Brett arrived home. Brett had initially been freaked out by her new zombie *Vogue* bride sister—had they drugged her? Brainwashed her?—but now she was only irritated by the whole situation.

"Are you a golf fan?" Brett's dad asked Mr. Cooper, taking a swig of freshly squeezed orange juice. Stuart Messerschmidt, whose favorite topic—tales of plastic surgery—had undoubtedly been banned by Bree, turned to his second favorite topic: sports. He looked more stressed out now than he had when the whole cast of the Rockettes came to him one November and demanded to be Botoxed for their first show.

Mr. Cooper swallowed a forkful of torte and nodded. "Yes, I am." He had on a pink Nautica button-down and a navy blue tie with tiny yellow sailboats. Apparently, Thanksgiving brunches were meant to be formal—when Bree had run into Brett in the upstairs hallway that morning, she'd marched Brett back to her bedroom and made her change out of her favorite orange Juicy Couture velour pants and black Rolling Stones T-shirt.

"Who's your favorite player?" Brett's dad asked, looking grateful that he'd found something to discuss. Brett's mom, in some kind of beige pantsuit that looked like something a paralegal would wear, squeezed his hand across the table.

"Favorite player?" Mr. Cooper looked perplexed. He glanced at his wife, as if relying on her to interpret.

"I think he means on television," Mrs. Cooper said helpfully. She sipped at her glass of sparkling water.

"Oh." Mr. Cooper's face darkened, and he looked at Mr. Messerschmidt like he was a child. "I don't watch golf. I *play* it."

Brett's dad's face fell and it was all Brett could do to keep from reaching across the table and smacking Mr. Cooper. She tried to think of a biting comment about golf but couldn't come up with anything.

"Dad, you like Tiger Woods." Willy spoke up, pushing the piece of caviar torte toward the edge of his plate. He, Brett noticed with relief, wasn't wearing a tie.

Mr. Cooper nodded, his eyes a pale green, the color of a dollar bill that had gone through the wash accidentally. "Indeed, I do."

"It's impossible not to love a player like that." Mr. Messerschmidt shook his head and let out a soft whistle. "But personally, I'm a John Daly fan myself. Gotta love a guy who can mix it up like that."

"I don't know him," Bree said primly, knowing full well who he was. She adjusted the white headband holding her hair in place.

"You know, the fat one who plays drunk and has an ex-con for a wife," Brett answered gleefully, watching a horrified look cloud Bree's face. Brett had always groaned when she came into the room and her dad was watching golf on the big screen, but now it kind of came in handy.

Mr. and Mrs. Cooper shared a glance and then quietly returned to their torte.

"Would anyone like another orange-glazed blueberry scone?" Mrs. Messerschmidt jumped to her feet and passed the tray of hardened pastries around the table. She sank back down, playing with the strand of pearls around her neck that Brett had never seen her wear before. She tended to prefer over-size necklaces with lots of beads and gold, for a kind of kooky, Home Shopping Network look.

"We're big race fans," Willy spoke up, trying to change the subject. Brett noticed that he smiled really sweetly at Bree, who had a constipated look on her face.

"Nascar?" Brett's dad asked, and Brett let a tiny giggle escape.

"*No*," Bree said, exasperated. She set down her fork. "Crew. You know, boat racing?"

Brett narrowed her eyes. She was pretty sure Bree knew nothing about boat racing and Brett only wished that *she* did so that she could put Bree in her place. Who was this Ann Taylor bore and what had she done with Brett's fun-loving sister?

"Dad went to school in New Haven," Willy continued, taking a big gulp of his mimosa, "so that's his team."

"Sherrie down the street went to college in New Haven, too." Brett's mom smiled, her catlike green eyes that Brett had inherited bright with forced cheer. Sherrie Inman was her mom's best friend, president of their local chapter of the ASPCA, where her mom got all their teacup Chihuahuas, and rotating secretary of the Neighborhood Watch.

"Oh?" Mr. Cooper perked up. "What year?"

Brett's mom crinkled her brow. "Not sure. She studied restaurant management, I think."

"I don't think so," Mrs. Cooper said, stifling a laugh.

Mrs. Messerschmidt blinked at the blatant rudeness of Mrs. Cooper's remark. "She certainly did." She sat up straighter in her chair.

"Mom." Bree spoke up calmly, her pale, polish-free nails clinking impatiently against her half-full glass of grapefruit juice. "Mrs. Inman went to Albertus Magnus College."

"That's right," Brett's mom said forcefully, not understanding what Bree was trying to intimate.

"Mr. Cooper went to *New Haven* . . ." Bree continued. Brett had to clench her hands into fists not to roll her eyes.

"Albertus Magnus is in New Haven," Brett's mom said, confused.

"Mom . . ." Brett leaned toward her mother and spoke in a loud stage whisper. "People say they went to New Haven when they mean they went to *Yale*." Bree shot her a look.

"How about that?" Brett's dad said, chuckling softly, trying to defuse Brett's passive-aggressive tone.

"I knew this girl who went to Yale," Brett continued, laying her fork across her uneaten torte. "Well, actually it was a sister of someone who goes to Waverly. She was studying drama—"

"Yale has a famous drama program," Mrs. Cooper interrupted.

"Jodie Foster went there," Bree jumped in.

"Anyway," Brett continued, "the girl's sister dropped out and moved to New York City and got into modeling. She was like a top model in Paris and Milan and London. Traveled all over the world." Brett picked up her fork to see if the Coopers would take the bait.

"I think it's quite common for actors to drop out of college to take advantage of other opportunities." Bree narrowed her eyes and stared at Brett, wondering where she was going with this.

"What's her name?" Willy asked innocently.

"I don't remember." Brett forked a piece of bland honeydew melon. "I only remember her because she died of AIDS."

Mrs. Cooper coughed into her tight little fist.

"I don't think it was a sexual thing," Brett assured her. "It was from sharing needles. She picked up a really bad heroin habit in New Haven."

Mr. Cooper groaned audibly and Brett pushed back from her plate, sufficiently pleased with her made-up story. "I left my medication upstairs," she announced, and left the table, the sound of Bree apologizing profusely in her wake.

Brett flopped down on her queen-size sleigh bed and flipped through a copy of *W* lying by her bedside, hoping to be gone long enough for brunch to be over. All she'd wanted was a giant bowl of Cap'n Crunch (her dad's favorite breakfast cereal.) Her stomach growled at the thought.

Brett froze when she heard footsteps down the hall, and she wondered if maybe Bree was coming up to apologize for being such a mega-bitch. But the sound of Mrs. Cooper letting out a soft squeal piqued Brett's curiosity and she cracked open the door. She spied the Coopers, who had inadvertently opened the door to the upstairs laundry room, the temporary home of the Teacup Chihuahuas. Brett had spent an hour curled up with them last night, after everyone else had gone to sleep—the poor things were lonely for her mother. All their matching Gucci coats were stuffed onto one of the shelves above the dryer.

"Are they *dog* breeders?" Mr. Cooper asked in a low voice as his wife quickly shut the door on the yelping dogs. One of them escaped—was it Tinkerbell?—and quickly shot down the stairs.

"How could they know anything about breeding?" Mrs. Cooper asked, her voice dripping with sarcasm. "I mean, really."

Mr. Cooper chuckled. "I suppose you're right."

"Did you notice the torte was store-bought?" Mrs. Cooper sighed, heading farther down the hallway toward the guest room they'd taken over. "I saw the pie tins in the trash when I tried to locate the wine cellar. I don't think they have one, by the way."

"A mercy for the wine," Mr. Cooper added.

"The sister is a problem child, can you tell?" Mrs. Cooper opened another door. "Here we are. I just need to lie down for a minute before going down again."

Brett clicked her door shut, her ears burning. A blind fury descended and she clenched her fists and stared at the series of black-and-white photographs hanging over her bed that she'd taken in Crete. These people were terrible—snobs of the worst order. Brett was reminded of how she'd felt the first time she set foot on Waverly Academy's campus and quickly realized that wearing brand-new designer clothes was not the thing to do. Rather, dresses that were vintage, designer jeans that had lost some of their color, slightly scuffed leather boots and bags—

that was the way to go. It was subtle, and Brett had quickly FedExed half of the new outfits she and her mom had bought at the Mall at Short Hills back home, taking the earliest opportunity to train it down to New York and shop the secondhand stores in Williamsburg.

How could her sister bring these terrible people into their family, let alone into their house? Brett immediately ran over to her closet and threw open the mirrored-glass door, searching for some of her old clothes she'd deemed not appropriate for Waverly. And she wasn't going to stop at clothing. She grabbed her silver Nokia, a plan forming.

If the Coopers thought she was a problem child now, just wait till they met her friends.

 **Owl**Net   Instant Message Inbox

BrettMesserschmidt: You watching football?

SebastianValenti: Nah, not til later. What're U up to, babe?

BrettMesserschmidt: Believe it or not, wondering if you'd be interested in coming over for T-Day dinner. Sorry for the late notice, but it's boring over here.

SebastianValenti: You serious?

BrettMesserschmidt: You were just going to watch TV, right? Thought you might want some real turkey + stuffing.

SebastianValenti: Wow. Thanks. Should I bring anything?

BrettMesserschmidt: Just yourself. We eat at 6. See you then!

17

A WAVERLY OWL ALWAYS PLAYS NICE—EVEN WHEN SHE WANTS TO PUSH SOMEONE'S FACE IN A SNOWBANK.

A weak light filtered in through the snow-covered windows, casting a gauzy haze over the living room. Jenny opened her eyes, blinking away sleep as she stared up at the unfamiliar modern glass and wire chandelier hanging over her head. It took her a minute to remember that she was in Yvonne Stidder's living room, but only a second more to remember that Casey was slumbering peacefully just inches away.

She pulled the down blanket Casey had given her—it smelled like lavender—tighter around her. The room was silent, as if the blizzard last night had muffled all the normal city sounds Jenny was used to.

Then she turned her eyes to another beautiful sight—Casey, lying next to her, his arm stretched out beneath her pillow, almost like his arm was around her. The whole night came back to her in a rush—she remembered falling asleep murmuring with Casey, the living room alive with whispered secrets and covert flirting from the pairs of sleeping bags curled up on the floor. Somewhere between telling Casey about her father and listening to stories about life at Union, Jenny had drifted off to the best sleep she'd had in months. When she woke up in the middle of the night for a glass of water, she'd brushed her teeth again, not wanting to wake up with terrible breath. And now, staring at Casey's perfect skin, just inches from his face, she was grateful that she'd managed to think ahead. A tickle ran down Jenny's arm and as she reached to scratch it, Casey opened his eyes.

"Morning," she whispered.

"Good morning." He smiled. His eyes looked like melted Hershey's kisses.

Jenny yawned, covering her mouth with her hand.

"Someone's still tired," Casey said.

"Actually, I slept really well." An unruly curl slipped from behind Jenny's ear, falling across her face. She hoped it looked bed-head sexy and not unwashed. "I felt like I was sleeping on a cloud."

Casey's eyes moved slowly across her face. She imagined she was waking up in some ski lodge in the Alps, completely snowbound, with nothing else to do besides keep warm. And then, Casey leaned in to kiss her. She knew it was going to happen before it did. She felt his lips touch hers in a kiss so soft she thought she might still be dreaming.

When she finally opened her eyes and pulled away, her heart beat loudly in her chest. It was too perfect. "That was nice."

"Nice? That was better than nice." Casey rubbed his eye with his free hand and plopped his head back down on his folded-up pillow. "You taste like strawberries."

Jenny giggled softly, thanking her strawberry-mint Crest. "You taste like beer."

"Ooh, sorry."

"I don't mind," she confessed.

The body in the sleeping bag on the floor next to them stirred and they both froze, not wanting to break the magic of the stillness around them.

"You know what I love?" Jenny whispered, turning on her back and staring at the ceiling. She folded her arm back under her head.

"Tell me."

"I love that yesterday when I woke up I had no idea that I'd end up at Yvonne's party, or sleeping on her couch, or meeting you, or . . ." She blushed as her voice trailed off.

"I had it planned right down to the kiss," Casey said matter-of-factly, touching his fingers to the freckles on Jenny's pale arm. She giggled.

"Isn't it so great we go to school so close? I could totally come visit you."

Casey covered his mouth as he yawned. "Sure," he said. "Who knows?"

Jenny flushed with embarrassment. *Here I go again*, she thought. She remembered what Tinsley had said about taking it slow, about just having a good time. That was just so hard. Was she really supposed to kiss Casey and try to force herself not to feel anything? Well, she could certainly try. After all, when had Tinsley ever led her astray before?

Ha.

Tinsley touched the wet ends of her hair, annoyed that she'd been near the end of the line of girls showering in the penthouse's three full bathrooms and a dipshit sophomore had already burned out the only hair dryer. Yvonne had promised to run to the Duane Reade around the corner and get another, but she hadn't made it any further than the kitchen before she was swept up in multiple conversations about the day's plans, the blizzard having seized the city overnight. Several proposals to "drink all day, eat pizza, and then drink all night" were floated, prompting Yvonne to take down everyone's pizza order. Everyone yelled out their favorite toppings until Yvonne, flustered, promised to order one of each.

Tinsley paused in the hallway, tugging her cream-colored French Connection slouch sweater on over her plain white tank top. A picture of Yvonne and what must have been her father (he had the same corn silk blond hair and thick glasses) caught her eye. It was on the field at Yankee Stadium, and a young and extra-dorky-looking Yvonne was shaking hands with a young Derek Jeter, the famous—and famously hot—shortstop. Tinsley's dad would have been impressed.

Julian appeared as if by magic next to her, wearing the same clothes he'd had on yesterday. Tinsley had ended up at the opposite end of the living room last night, conscious of Julian playing cards with Yvonne's brother and his friends. At least he wasn't curled up on a sofa with Sleigh. He glanced at Tinsley and touched the frame of the picture, straightening it. "You're not a baseball fan, are you?"

"Why so surprised?" Tinsley stuck her hands in the pockets of her skinny black Citizens. "Can't girls like baseball?" She stuck her chin out toward him. She didn't like baseball at all, but she kind of wanted to prove to him that he didn't have her completely pegged.

"You're just a wealth of surprises, aren't you?" Julian crossed his arms and leaned against the door frame.

Tinsley ran her socked toe against the dark hardwood floor. "Although, in the spirit of full disclosure, I'm actually more of a hot baseball *player* fan."

Julian laughed, a nice, full-body laugh that gave Tinsley tingles. It felt good to make him laugh again. "Did you sleep well?"

"Like a log," she lied. "The most comfortable floor on the Upper East Side." She smiled to let him know she wasn't complaining and he returned the smile. *Yes.* Tinsley could feel things falling into place. "So, what are your plans today?"

Julian shrugged. "It looks terrible out there." He turned and looked out the window overlooking a snow-covered Eightieth Street. Overnight, three feet of snow had fallen across Manhattan, the biggest snowfall the city had gotten in years, and a giant yellow plow was working its way down the street. The parked cars were mysterious-looking mounds of snow.

"Are you kidding?" Tinsley asked softly, touching her fingers to the windowpane. A petite woman with four black Labs on leashes trundled through the unplowed sidewalk, letting the dogs drag her toward the park. "It's *beautiful* out." She turned back to Julian. "We should go sledding in the park?"

Julian ran a hand through his longish hair, considering the offer.

"Don't say no," Tinsley added, hoping it didn't sound like begging.

"Yeah, okay." He turned toward her. "You've got mittens?"

Tinsley's heart did a victory dance in her chest. "Of course."

The plasma TV on the living room wall switched on, and whoever had the remote dialed up SportsCenter. A preview of the Detroit Lions/Green Bay Packers game joined the cacophony of voices in the room, but Tinsley couldn't think about anyone but Julian. She followed him to the coat closet and he immediately pulled out her gray wool Michael Kors belted trench. *He remembers*, she thought.

"Where are you kids off to?" Sleigh appeared in the doorway to the kitchen, tilting her braided blond head against the door frame and sipping a glass of orange juice, wearing the same hippie shirt she'd had on yesterday. Tinsley was instantly grateful she had her suitcase with her.

We *aren't off anywhere*, Tinsley thought, and almost verbalized the sentiment. But she knew if she were to win Julian back, she couldn't start off by sniping at Sleigh. Tinsley still couldn't believe that she'd materialized after all these years. It was like one of those creepy movies where someone comes back from the dead.

"We're going sledding in Central Park," Julian answered as he slipped on a puffy olive green jacket.

"Awesome! Mind if I tag along?"

Tinsley's mind faltered as she laced up her Ugg Adirondack boots, searching for the right thing to say that would let Sleigh know she wasn't welcome without sounding like she was being a bitch—which, of course, she was.

"Sure," Julian answered before Tinsley could say anything. He tugged on a pair of thick black gloves. "Grab your coat."

In the elevator, Sleigh yammered on about some snowboarding trip to Telluride she'd taken with another "homeschooled" friend—"It was like our spring break"—and how cool the hippies in Colorado were, and how she'd learned Telemark skiing from Ty, one of the hot ski instructors.

New leaf, Tinsley reminded herself. *You're turning over a new leaf. You are a much nicer person now, and stupid Sleigh Monroe-Hill is not going to fuck things up for you.*

"Fun!" Tinsley commented, apropos of nothing, in the spirit of good cheer.

And so, the three traipsed through the snowdrifts, stamping their feet on the odd sidewalk that had actually been shoveled, the crisp late-morning air cold in their lungs as they made their way toward the park. Tinsley wrapped her black scarf around her neck to ward off the chill, amazed at how Sleigh left open the top of her Urban Outfitters–looking puke-brown jacket, her neckline exposed to the elements. *Goddamn hippie chick*, Tinsley thought. She sent a death stare at the back of Sleigh's head as Sleigh put a hand-knit pink mitten on Julian's arm. "Hold on," she said. "I'll be right back."

Sleigh ducked into a corner bodega. The electric light from

the neon Boar's Head sign reflected in the untrampled snow. Tinsley jammed her gloved hands into her pockets, shivering.

"So," she ventured, "how do you know Sleigh?"

"She's friends with my roommate Kevin's older sister," Julian answered, kicking up a cloud of snow into the frosty air. "I've hung out with her a few times. She's cool."

"Yeah," Tinsley answered involuntarily. She stomped a circle in the snow to keep warm, her Uggs leaving perfect imprints. She paused, staring up at Julian. Snowflakes were starting to fall again, landing on his oatmeal-colored hat. The city was silent around her. Suddenly, Tinsley didn't give a fuck what Sleigh did. "We used to be roommates."

"Really?" Julian arched an eyebrow, as if he detected some sarcasm, but Tinsley stared through the glass of the bodega instead. "She's a good person."

This last bit stung Tinsley's already frozen skin. *Good person* was high praise for Julian. A good person? Does a good person throw someone's brand-new iMac full of her un-backed-up homework out the fourth-floor window? No.

As if on cue, Sleigh reappeared, her hands balancing three white cups with cardboard slipcovers on them. "I thought we might want some hot cocoa." She smiled sweetly, her striped stocking hat tugged down over her forehead.

"Awesome," Julian said, taking a cup. Steam escaped out of the tiny hole in the plastic top.

"I got you mint." Sleigh handed Tinsley the cup with the black *X* markered on the lid. "I remembered that used to be your favorite."

Tinsley tried not to puke. Right. Sleigh knew her for three months and remembered how she liked her cocoa? Tinsley forced a smile. "Yeah, thanks," she managed to say. She wanted to drench Sleigh in the scalding cocoa, to melt away the fake veneer so Julian could see how awful she was underneath. She searched Sleigh's eyes for any sign of irony, for some flicker of the old, vindictive roommate she used to know—had she put Tabasco in Tinsley's X-marked cup? Arsenic? Laxatives? Tinsley remembered how Sleigh had poured her Frédéric Fekkai shampoo and conditioner down the toilet—but all she saw was an angelic-looking freckled face.

Sleigh took another sip of her cocoa, licking her lips like a child tasting ice cream for the first time. "Isn't this, like, the perfect day?" She scooped a handful of snow off a buried mailbox and tossed it good-naturedly toward Tinsley, who giggled hesitantly in response. Was it possible that Sleigh had truly changed? Had she really let go of her old grudge?

Tinsley took a sip of her cocoa. It tasted amazing, but not quite as amazing as the sight of Julian grinning at her with that playful, mischievous, adorable face of his. She scooped up a handful of snow and slung it in his direction. She could out-nice Sleigh any day. It would just take some effort.

OwlNet   Instant Message Inbox

CallieVernon: TC, where the hell R U?

CallieVernon: You abandon me at Yvonne's? REALLY???

CallieVernon: Seriously, where'd you go?

CallieVernon: WTF? Where is everyone?

JennyHumphrey: Ice skating in the Park. With Casey. Come join us!

CallieVernon: Sorry. Don't need to break my ankle before I
see EZ. Maybe I'll get a mani-pedi instead.

JennyHumphrey: K! Later!

A WAVERLY OWL KNOWS THAT WHEN IT COMES TO CUTE BOYS, IT'S BEST TO WASTE NOT, WANT NOT.

Callie sat alone in Yvonne Stidder's sunny breakfast nook late Thursday morning, listening to the noises of Xbox in the other room and sipping the awful decaf Sanka she'd found at the back of a drawer in the kitchen, the watery coffee tepid in her mouth. Her stomach barked with hunger, but her thoughts were so wrapped up in meeting Easy later on top of the Empire State Building. She picked at the powdered sugar doughnut from the box someone had brought back from the bakery on the corner and gazed out the window at all the powdered snow.

Callie glanced at the dangling antique gold watch on her wrist, a Sweet Sixteen present from her father, the minutes ticking by with agonizing slowness. How the hell was she supposed to make it until eight o'clock? The whole day stretched out before her like a desert—somehow, the past four weeks without

Easy seemed like nothing compared to the endless stretch of time between them now. It was totally unfair of Tinsley and Jenny to desert her like this—what she really needed right now was someone to take her mind off the wait . . . or a trip to a spa. She'd called around to all the beauty salons in the area, hoping to squeeze in a relaxing mani-pedi, but everything was closed for the holiday. Plus, it looked damn cold out there, reminding her oh-too-painfully of her time out in the Maine woods at the rehab detention facility her mom had promised her was a spa. She swallowed another mouthful of Sanka and then tipped the cup into the sink.

"I could use some of that." Ellis, the cute guy she'd spent an hour talking to last night, yawned as he strode into the kitchen, his dark socked feet sliding across the granite floor. He massaged his neck. "I had to sleep like a pretzel."

"Ouch." Callie winced sympathetically. "Sanka's probably not the answer, though. You need Starbucks."

"Good diagnosis." Ellis laughed. "Wanna join me?" He leaned against one of the breakfast table chairs. His short, dark blond hair was wet from the shower and he smelled like shaving cream.

"Is Starbucks open on Thanksgiving?" Callie suddenly felt self-conscious that she'd just thrown on her old gray Juicy Couture V-neck sweater over a plain black T-shirt and her boring black stretch Banana Republic pants. She planned to dress up later for Easy, but needed an outfit to kill time in the meantime, and now she felt frumpy—even though Ellis was wearing the same sweater he'd had on last night.

"This wouldn't be America if they weren't."

Callie bit her lip. They were both in relationships. So what was the harm in sitting in a crowded, commercialized coffee shop, sipping a latte ten times stronger than the stale Sanka she'd been drinking?

Next to a cute boy who was not her boyfriend.

"Sure," she agreed, a little guiltily. Thankfully, Tinsley wasn't there to see her leaving with Ellis. And if Tinsley hadn't ditched her in the first place, Callie wouldn't even be hanging out with him. Tinsley wouldn't understand, and Callie didn't want any gossip—especially on this day, the best day of all days.

They bundled up and headed out into the street. The sidewalks, only partially plowed, were surprisingly filled with busy New Yorkers, bags of last-minute groceries or boxes from local bakeries in their hands. They pushed through the front door of the closest Starbucks, which was less than a block away. All the seats were taken, the tables filled with young men on laptops or women reading magazines. Callie was suddenly gripped by an overwhelming sense of loneliness. It just seemed so sad that these people had nowhere better to be on Thanksgiving than Starbucks. Then again, she was here too.

Ellis leaned toward her with concern. "Are you okay?" The cappuccino machines whirred behind the counter as he handed her the grande nonfat vanilla latte she'd ordered.

"Yeah." Callie held up the steaming paper cup and inhaled the smell. What was wrong with her? "I think I just . . . I don't know. I'm jittery, I guess. I can't believe I have to wait all day to see Easy." She took a sip of her latte, the hot liquid burning her throat.

"I bet." Ellis nodded sympathetically as he emptied a packet of sugar into his coffee. "You just need something to take your mind off the wait." He buttoned up his black double-breasted Diesel wool coat. "Come on."

Half an hour later, they emerged from the subway. Callie was grateful that Ellis knew exactly where they were going, since she was completely lost whenever she glanced at one of the multicolored Metro maps. She'd ridden the subway only a handful of times in her life, and the number 6 line, with its sticky seats and newspaper-strewn floors, was pretty gross. But it was almost worth the ride just for the moment when she and Ellis emerged from the underground station. An enormous, Gothic-looking structure loomed in front of them.

Ellis glanced at her. "You ever been across the Brooklyn Bridge?"

"You can walk across it?" Callie asked, surprised. Cars zoomed over the enormous suspension bridge in front of them, horns honking and lights flashing. "It's not, like, dangerous?"

"No, it's totally safe," Ellis said confidently. "Tons of people walk across it every day." He led Callie up a wide ramp that turned into the elevated pedestrian walkway, looking down on the cars speeding by below. The wind whipped through Callie's hair, and she forgot to be nervous as she spotted the wavering image of a city of skyscrapers, reflected in the dark blue, almost black water of the East River.

"Wow." Callie stopped and leaned against the railing.

A young couple in NYU sweats jogged past them, pushing a fancy baby stroller. "We're so high up." She started to turn around, to look back at the city, but Ellis put his gloved hands on her shoulders.

"Don't look back yet."

"What?" Callie stepped slightly closer to him. "Why not?"

"Trust me. It's better if you wait. The view is amazing from further out." Ellis pointed ahead of them at the towering brick arches. Millions of cables swept from the tops of the towers to the sides of the bridge, like a giant metal spiderweb. They walked for a few minutes without saying anything. The loud, rhythmic sounds of the traffic below, combined with the movement of the water, had a calming effect on Callie. The more steps she took, the more she started to feel grateful—for the sunny blue sky above her, the warmth of the latte through her blue cashmere gloves, the—

"Now," Ellis instructed, tugging on Callie's coat for her to stop. She turned around quickly, and her stomach dropped at the sight of lower Manhattan. The smooth glass of the skyscrapers glinted in the sunlight, the pointed tops reaching up into the clouds. A gust of wind blew, sending Callie's hair flying in her face. But even through the wispy strands of blond, the view was incredible.

"Wow," Callie repeated, her heart beating faster. "It's so beautiful." She couldn't take her eyes off the buildings, which almost seemed miniature from their high perch. She opened her mouth to thank Ellis for bringing her here, but something cold slammed into her neck.

She spun around to see a couple of preteen boys in puffy North Face jackets aiming snowballs directly at them. "They just hit me!" she sputtered.

"Then what are you waiting for?" Ellis was already scooping a handful of snow from the snowbank at the edge of the walkway, packing it into a tight ball. He sent a perfectly aimed snowball directly into one kid's stomach.

"War!" The kids shrieked gleefully and scrambled to pack more snowballs. And before she knew it, Callie was digging her hands into the dirty snow bank, not even worrying about ruining her gloves.

Pilgrim Hill in Central Park was a crowd of brightly colored parkas on a brilliant white bed of snow, little kids in red and pink jackets scampering around, their cheerful parents chasing them like ants crawling through sugar. A crafty vendor was selling plastic flying saucer sleds, fifteen dollars apiece, and dozens of kids with inflatable toboggans flew recklessly down the hill, careening into a wide, snowy field. Sleigh broke out a fifty and sprang for three saucers before Tinsley could even offer to pay. The vendor eyed the fifty to see if it was real while Tinsley retied the lace of her boot.

"I've never sledded," Julian announced, glancing around at the kids waddling like penguins in their full-body snowsuits. "Can you believe that?"

"You West Coast boys." Sleigh shook her head in disbelief, her blond hair falling out of her messy braid and into her face as she led the way toward the top of the hill. "I used to bring my little brother here all the time when we were kids."

"That's cute." Julian lifted his saucer over his head, like a shield. "I bet it was totally fun growing up near this."

Tinsley watched this back-and-forth, remembering how annoying it was that Sleigh always managed to turn every single conversation back to her. Tinsley knew she had to jump in before Sleigh started talking about her fucking favorite color or something. "When I was working on my documentary in South Africa, I tried to explain snow to the kids there"—she liked how this made her sound like Mother Teresa—"and their eyes got about as wide as these sleds."

Julian laughed, satisfying Tinsley's need for attention. "That's crazy." The three of them moved just in time to avoid being hit by a little boy who'd accidentally slid down the wrong side of the hill. A stockbroker-looking guy in a long gray wool coat and a pair of knee-high Hunter wellies chased after him.

"I know exactly what you mean," Sleigh countered. "I used to volunteer at the Children's Crisis Center in Florida—this really awful place where they put kids who have been taken away from their parents by the cops—"

"That sucks," Julian said. He pulled the sticker off the bottom of his sled. Tinsley shook some snow off the top of her boots. Volunteering? Right. On the *one* day she wasn't sunbathing at her parents' West Palm Beach mansion.

"Yeah, right?" Sleigh continued without missing a beat. "These kids were so great. They had no idea what was going on. And my job was just to entertain them. You know, to take their mind off things. They could be totally traumatized, but when you started telling them a really great story or something, you should have seen the looks on these kids' faces. It was totally worth it to make them smile."

"Wow." Julian hiked up the last bit of the hill.

"Yeah, it's amazing," Tinsley said, jumping in. "Families are so different in South Africa. It's like a totally different way of living, not like we have here." She could feel herself floundering. "I remember once, at Christmastime, I asked this girl in one of the villages where we were filming if she was ready for presents—"

"Do they have Christmas in South Africa?" Sleigh piped up.

"Not officially," Tinsley answered earnestly. "But there's a mix of people and they all know about Christmas." She smiled at Julian to reassert her storytelling credibility. "Anyway, the little girl said she didn't have any presents this year and so I got the crew together and we pooled everything we had—combs, key chains, crossword puzzle books, colored pencils—just anything we could scrounge up and we wrapped them in newspaper for this little girl and her two sisters. You can't imagine the look on their faces."

"Wow," Julian said. "Very cool. I'll bet that little girl will never forget that Christmas." His breath floated out in front of him and he smiled at Tinsley, maybe seeing her in a new light. At least, she hoped.

"That's just like the time I was building houses in the Dominican Republic!" Before Sleigh could plunge into another endless story about building wells, Tinsley tossed her sled down and looked down the hill, crisscrossed with ruts and bootprints of all sizes by now.

"Last one to the bottom is a rotten egg!" Tinsley dropped on her knees. The plastic sled felt cold through her jeans. The sled spun clockwise and Tinsley pushed off violently, taking a wide lead on Sleigh and Julian, who pounced on their sleds after her. The three plummeted down the slope, scattering a group of kids who were loafing at the bottom, Tinsley in first, Sleigh in second, and Julian stalled a few feet from the bottom, his sled squirting out from under him.

"That was crazy!" Sleigh shrieked wildly, and Tinsley actually started to wonder about her sanity. It wasn't totally hard to believe that her "mental health break" from Waverly had led to more serious problems, like schizophrenia. "Feel my heart racing," Sleigh grabbed Julian's hand and pressed it to her chest, as if he could feel something beneath her thick, butt-ugly jacket.

"Mine too," Julian said, removing his hand quickly and putting it on his chest. "That was excellent."

"Best two out of three," Sleigh said, sprinting back up the hill.

Tinsley followed, with Julian in tow. A snowball fight broke out near the top of the hill and a cold spiral whizzed by Tinsley's head, barely missing her.

"That kid almost nailed you," Julian said, panting from the incline.

"Good thing he's seven." Tinsley laughed. "Or I might have to smack him."

The results of the second race were exactly the same as the first, even though she kept hoping Sleigh would somehow plow into a tree and leave her alone with Julian. Being around her again was suffocating, and the nice thing was getting tiresome. She needed a quick escape to gather her thoughts. Then she remembered Olesia's, the tiny bakery with croissants that melted in your mouth, just across the park.

"I'll be right back," Tinsley said, dropping her sled at her feet.

"Where are you going?" Julian asked. He patted the snow off his jeans.

"You can both race for second place." She clomped through the knee-deep snow in the direction of Olesia's. She was actually hungry, but she wasn't fetching the buttery pastries to sate the growling in her stomach. Two could play at hospitality. The warm air inside Olesia's blasted her face as she surveyed the fully stocked display case. She upgraded her order from regular croissants to chocolate croissants. Why not force-feed Sleigh a few extra calories, too?

Twenty minutes later, Tinsley found Sleigh and Julian practically where she'd left them, though Julian was standing off to the side, the sleds stacked in a pile next to him, while Sleigh chased two identical twins dressed in matching pink snowsuits. The twins galloped through the snow, shrieking as Sleigh pretended to get them. Weren't their parents worried about some crazy teenager playing with their kids?

"Whatcha got there?" Julian asked, pointing at the bag in Tinsley's hand.

"Chocolate croissants." Tinsley opened the bag and Julian peered into it.

"How sweet of you," Sleigh said, winded, the twins on her heels. She turned suddenly and the twins shrieked. "Are you hungry?"

"Those are for us . . ." Tinsley started to say before realizing that taking pastries from two small children would probably disqualify her from being a "good person." "But you guys can, uh, have them." She reluctantly handed the bag to one of the twins, who snatched it greedily.

The slow burn inside Tinsley simmered dangerously close to the boiling point. Her eyes misted and she blinked away the hate she felt for Sleigh as the twins ripped into the bag.

"Do you know how to build a snowman?" Julian asked the twins, bending down to their level.

"Snowman!" The twins shouted in unison. They threw the croissants to the ground and followed Julian toward a large snowdrift that had accumulated under a stand of trees.

Tinsley bit her lip, eyeing the ruined pastries. In one swift movement, Sleigh moved next to Tinsley, both of them watching Julian and the twins.

"I know exactly what you're doing," Sleigh said menacingly, her voice the one Tinsley remembered from freshman year, absent of all rainbows and sunshine. "You stole a guy from me once, and I'm not going to let it happen again. Remember what I did to all your stuff? Watch your ass or I'll do something twice as bad."

Tinsley's jaw dropped. She'd never doubted her ability to

kick Sleigh's ass—she'd come close freshman year—but the sudden change that had come over Sleigh freaked her out and she stood mute, wishing Julian could somehow hear.

Sleigh plastered the smile back on her face. "Did Julian tell you I'm thinking of coming back to Waverly? It was his idea. So maybe I'll see you around campus." She strode off in the direction of Julian and the twins, helping them with the snowman.

Tinsley stared in disbelief. Okay, change of plans. There was clearly no way to out-nice Sleigh. The only other option was to expose her as the manipulative bitch she was.

And that sounded like a hell of a lot more fun.

19

A WAVERLY OWL IS HOSPITABLE TO ALL GUESTS—
EVEN THOSE WHO PREFER ANIMAL PRINTS.

The Messerschmidts were suffering through a long, boring history of the Coopers of Greenwich when the doorbell chimed to the tune of "Born in the U.S.A." Brett had noticed that her mom had changed the chime to a few innocuous strands of Beethoven, but Brett had changed it back. She could see the Coopers wince visibly.

"I'll get it!" Brett leapt to her feet. Her cropped black C&C California ballet shirt slid off her left shoulder, the silky yellow strap of her Paul & Joe camisole bra bright against her pale skin. The shirt fell just below her navel and an inch of skin peeked out above her Dolce & Gabbana leopard-print skirt—a gift from her mother for her birthday last year. Her bare feet with their bright pink polished toes (Bourjois Pink Flamingo) padded across the cold marble floor of the foyer, and she was thankful to be released from the stuffy front room where the

Coopers and her parents had gathered for afternoon tea. Afternoon tea! Unreal.

She swung open the heavy door to find Sebastian standing in the doorway, his black leather jacket open at the collar despite the gusts of wind sweeping snow across the Messerschmidts' expansive front yard. The gold chain around his neck glinted in the sunlight, and a cloud of Drakkar Noir blew into her face. But for once, Brett didn't mind the cheesy eighties cologne. In fact, she kind of liked it, at least for her immediate purposes.

"Hey," she said, suddenly shy. "Come on in."

"Wow." Sebastian shook his head, his eyes taking in her bare feet and making their way up her body. "Is this how you dress up for every holiday?"

Brett self-consciously hoisted her shirt back up on her shoulder, rolling her eyes at Sebastian. "Only the special ones." He tore his dark eyes off her and surveyed the Messerschmidts' sky-high foyer, shaking his head, impressed.

"Man, your whole family is into jungle prints?" he asked, staring into the front media room. "That's hot." Brett had "spilled" water on the beige slipcovers Bree had used to cover up their zebra-print chairs, pulling them off with glee. The seven Teacup Chihuahuas ran yipping into the foyer, jumping excitedly at Sebastian's legs. She'd freed the dogs a few hours ago, playing on her mother's sympathies: *They're so lonely and confused, locked up in that tiny room*, she'd cajoled, until her mom had relented.

"I guess it's genetic." Brett hung up Sebastian's jacket in the hall closet, right next to the Coopers' camel-hair coats. She

smiled widely as he followed her into the sitting room, inter-
rupting Mrs. Cooper's monologue on her family's Cavalier King
Charles spaniels.

"Everyone, this is Sebastian," Brett announced, gesturing
toward Sebastian like a game show host revealing a prize. "He's
a friend from Waverly."

Brett introduced him around, noting the coolness of the
Coopers and the warmness of her own parents toward him. She
felt a sudden surge of emotion—her parents were good people;
they just liked big shiny things.

"And that's my sister, Bree." She pointed to Bree and
Willy, who were camped out on the love seat. Bree cradled her
mug of chamomile tea, legs crossed delicately at the ankle.
Her flowered dress rose about an inch above her knee, and
she quickly tugged it down. "Er, Anna." Brett corrected herself, hitting her palm lightly against her forehead. She stage-
whispered, "Sorry," to Bree before continuing. "And that's her
boyfriend, Willy."

"Cool, man," Sebastian said to Willy, shaking his hand. He
nodded at Bree, taking Brett's confusion about her own sister's
name in stride.

"Would you like some tea?" Brett asked innocently, folding
her hands behind her back. Mr. Cooper set his teacup on the
leopard-print coaster that Brett had helpfully retrieved from
the hall closet.

"Um, yeah." Sebastian glanced around at the others. "Or, do
you have any Red Bull or Gatorade or anything like that?"

Brett watched Mrs. Cooper as she stared at Sebastian's carefully sculpted black hair. It looked like he had applied extra gel for the occasion.

"It's something, isn't it?" Brett asked boldly, following Mrs. Cooper's gaze. She touched Sebastian's hair and he flinched, waving off her hand.

"Hey." He frowned in annoyance. He actually looked kind of handsome in a pair of black jeans and a pressed white button-down. Even if it was opened two buttons too low at the neck. "I just did it."

"I wasn't staring at his hair." Mrs. Cooper had turned crimson. She picked up her teacup and swirled the tea, pretending to be engrossed with a speck of something on her linen pants.

"Don't worry. All the girls do," Brett said confidentially to Mrs. Cooper, as if they were sharing sex secrets at the beauty parlor. It was kind of fun to shock her—and a little too easy.

Sebastian smoothed the spot where Brett had threatened to touch his hair. He gave her a funny look. "Is that so?"

"I'm afraid I don't know what Red Bull is." Brett's mom scrambled to her feet, a worried look on her face.

"It's like this caffeine energy drink," Sebastian said helpfully. "Any kind of soda is fine, though."

"I'll get it," Brett offered. She skipped to the kitchen and was back in a flash with a glass of ice and a can of Mountain Dew for Sebastian, who was perched at the edge of a hard-backed wooden chair. She almost passed out with delight when she heard him talking about how hard it was to replace the gearshift in his Mustang with an eight ball.

"I've got this uncle who owns a pool hall," Sebastian said, taking the glass from Brett and setting it on the end table. "Hey, thanks." He sipped the soda appreciatively.

Brett grabbed Sebastian's hand and tugged him over to the sofa, pulling him down next to her. He stared at her small hand in his, and once they collapsed into the cushy, oversize cheetah-print pillows Brett had rescued from the media room, she quickly let go. "You're just in time," she said. "We were about to look at the old family photo album."

"*Brett*." Bree's green eyes darkened. "Don't be ridiculous. We don't want to bore everyone."

Brett shooed her sister's hand off the antique trunk and opened the lid. Out of the flotsam of crushed board games, old television remotes, and VHS home videos, she triumphantly pulled a thick photo album with a pink furry cover. "I'm sure Willy would like to see how adorable you were as a kid," Brett said, honeying her voice for effect.

"You bet." Willy sat forward, affable as ever, leaning the elbows of his thick marbled wool Nautica sweater on the knees of his khakis.

Brett flipped open the photo album. "Here's a great one," she sighed, pulling out the well-remembered photo of a pre-teen Bree and a kindergarten-aged Brett both dressed up as Madonna for Halloween, their blond wigs teased into wild hairstyles, wearing matching black lace tops over red cropped tanks and flared denim miniskirts. "We won a contest at the mall—remember? We sang 'Material Girl' and you threw your white lace glove into the audience." She glanced at her sister, who scowled angrily in reply. "They went wild," she whispered to Willy as she handed off the picture.

"I barely remember that." Bree crossed her arms primly across her chest, not looking at the Coopers. "It was a long time ago."

"It's really cute." Willy squeezed Bree's cable-knit-stockinged knee. "I didn't know you were into Madonna."

"That's awesome." Sebastian nudged Brett. "I dressed up as Michael Jackson once. You should've seen my moonwalk." Brett couldn't help giggling.

"You have to remember this," Brett said gleefully. "This is from one of those booths at Disney World. Where they make fake magazine covers with your picture?" She looked at the Coopers, as if they ever would have done such a thing, as she pulled out the picture of Bree, hand on her hip, on the cover of *Cosmopolitan*. The headline read, *Bree Messerschmidt: Sixteen-Year-Old Goddess*.

"Let's see," Willy said eagerly. He held out his hand and Brett passed him the picture. "I am so framing this," he chided Bree, grinning.

Sebastian burst out laughing, pointing at the picture of an eight-year-old Brett, wearing all black and waving a guitar over her head, on the cover of *Rolling Stone*. "You totally have a rock star complex, don't you?"

Mrs. Messerschmidt, most likely remembering that on the next page were the pictures of her and Mr. Messerschmidt on the cover of *Fortune*, hopped to her feet and grabbed the photo album away from Brett.

"That's enough," Brett's mom said firmly. But Brett could tell she wouldn't have minded the embarrassing photo tour if it hadn't been for the Coopers. "What would we have to look at later?"

"Hey, Dad, what kind of work do you think *Madonna's* had done?" Brett asked innocently, knowing it was her dad's favorite topic.

Stuart Messerschmidt's face lit up, and he leaned back in his armchair and crossed his hands over his stomach. "I'd say at the very least, she's had a series of Botox injections—a woman of her age? No forehead lines?" He chuckled merrily. "And most likely a mini facelift and neck lift, because she just looks too damn good to be a natural fifty."

Mr. Cooper cleared his throat, signaling his desire for a change of subject.

"My dad's a miracle worker." Brett stretched her legs out in front of her and thought she caught Mr. Cooper staring at her skirt. Repressed bastard probably liked it. A trio of Chihuahuas scampered into the front room—Curly, Larry, and Princess, from the look of it. "He's worked on everyone in the neighborhood."

"Oh!" Mrs. Cooper gasped, lifting her feet after Princess skittered over them. Sebastian gave a little whistle and the dogs immediately ran to him, jumping into his lap and trying to lick his face with their little pink tongues.

"Brett, why don't you help me check on the turkey?" her mother pleaded. "Dad shouldn't be so modest." Brett ignored her mom and scooped up Curly, who responded by licking Brett's fingers. The soft, warm tongue tickled, and Brett giggled. "The whole block has been smoothed out by your Botox injections, or nipped and tucked and polished. We should be voted the hottest neighborhood in New Jersey!"

Sebastian snorted. "Dude, that's too funny."

Brett glanced at Mrs. Cooper, who looked apoplectic. "And what's-her-name, with that . . ." She kept her eyes on Mrs. Cooper, particularly the loose flesh under her chin. "What did you call it?" She grabbed the loose skin on her neck.

"My mom has one of those," Sebastian spoke up, scratching Princess under her chin. "She hates it. She moved down to Miami." He looked around the room. "My parents are divorced. Anyway, she says no one in Miami has one. I forget what they call it too."

"It's a wattle," Brett's dad said, staring into his teacup.

"Right," Sebastian said, holding his Mountain Dew out as though he were making a toast. "A wattle."

Brett kept her eyes on Mrs. Cooper, who averted her gaze. Of course she was absolutely dying to ask Brett's dad if he could do something about her wattle but was too uptight to open her mouth.

"Can we change the subject?" Bree pleaded. "Please?"

A wave of satisfaction came over Brett as she watched her sister squirm along with the Coopers. Served them right. She could sense that her parents were amused by the whole thing, though they'd never let on.

"Where did you get these coasters?" Sebastian asked suddenly, taking up one of the leopard-print tiles Brett had unearthed from a shoebox stashed in the pantry. "They rock."

Mrs. Messerschmidt glanced at Bree, unsure what to say. "Our interior designer . . . had them custom made for me." She glanced apologetically at the Coopers. "It was a phase I went through."

"Well, I might have to get her number. These would make a great Christmas present for my mom." Sebastian was still stroking Princess on his lap. He turned to Brett's father. "Sir, I have to say, that plasma television hanging in your front room has to be one of the most beautiful pieces of art I've ever seen."

Mr. Messerschmidt's face brightened immediately. "Son, sometimes I stare at it, and I think it's more beautiful than a Monet—and that's when it's turned off!" He broke into his trademark wheezing, red-faced laugh and pounded Sebastian on the back.

The Coopers looked so mortified, they almost spilled their tea. Brett leaned her elbow against the cheetah-print pillow, her knee brushing Sebastian's. He raised his can of Mountain Dew and banged it against her can of Diet Coke. The student had become the teacher.

OwlNet   Instant Message Inbox

BrandonBuchanan: Where the fuck R U? Dunderdorf's on his third story about goats!

HeathFerro: Smokin' a J out back. Need something to keep me sane.

BrandonBuchanan: What about ME?

HeathFerro: I'll leave the roach out here for you. Keep your effing panties on.

A WAVERLY OWL KNOWS THAT SOMEONE IS ALWAYS WATCHING.

Tinsley opened the sliding glass door to the roof deck to let in a breath of fresh air. Yvonne's apartment was stale with warm bodies huddled around the plasma TV, watching an *America's Next Top Model* marathon and passing around someone's weed. A landslide of snow tumbled down on her sock-covered feet, and she squealed softly.

"Hey, close the door!" someone yelled from the living room. "You're letting all the smoke out!"

Tinsley inhaled a long breath of fresh air before sliding the door shut. Her afternoon frolicking in the snow with Julian like little kids would have been storybook perfect, if only Sleigh Monroe-Hill hadn't been glued to Julian's side the entire time. The glass door was like a mirror in the darkness, reflecting the image of Tinsley in her swinging black Lauren Conrad mini-dress, the soft jersey fabric and the sliced bell sleeves giving her a much more sophisticated hippie look than Sleigh's home-less-girl rags. *Take that*, Tinsley thought, spinning on her wool tights.

"Pizza's here!" Yvonne came skidding out of the dining room, where she and some of her dorky friends were lighting candles for what they kept calling the "Thanksgiving feast." Tinsley glanced around the room, looking for Julian. About half the guests had trickled home to their families that morning, but the other half—people the snowstorm had stranded in the city, or whose families had abandoned them like Tinsley's—had stuck around.

Even though she'd spent the last hour curled in front of the fireplace in Yvonne Stidder's cozy library, the only room in the penthouse that didn't feature any stainless steel, Tinsley couldn't shake the creepy feeling she'd gotten during her afternoon outing. Sleigh Monroe-Hill had to be the fakest person on earth, and it gave her chills that she had manipulated Julian into actually thinking she was nice. Tinsley was dying to pull Julian into an empty room and whisper to him all the terrible things Sleigh had done, even tell him how she'd threatened Tinsley just an hour ago, but that was probably exactly what Sleigh wanted.

Yvonne managed to gather the dozen or so stranded Owls in the dining room, the air filled with the delicious smell of pepperoni, sausage, and mushrooms. Her brother and a few of his friends, hunting for the football game on the living room television, grabbed three boxes of pizza for themselves over Yvonne's protests.

"Sit wherever." Yvonne, looking vaguely like a librarian in a ribbed brown turtleneck dress with a thin black belt around the waist, took a seat at the head of the carved walnut dining table. Red votive candles flickered in small bowls of water around the table, casting a romantic glow on everyone's faces. Tinsley waited for Sleigh to take her seat—at the other end of the table, predictably—and was chagrined when Julian sat next to her. Did she have him chained to her? Julian was listening to a story Sleigh was telling about her mother making her read *War and Peace*—and how *grateful* she was for the experience. Tinsley grabbed the chair across from him, next to Rifat Jones, as if to show Julian this wasn't a competition.

"It looks pretty in here, Yvonne," Tinsley spoke up, smoothing out her dress against her thick black tights. "You guys did a great job."

Yvonne blushed furiously and slid into a seat on the other side of Rifat, whose mother was an ambassador for Somalia and was attending the president's Thanksgiving dinner in Washington, D.C. "Thank you," she squeaked at Tinsley. "Quick, everyone, dig in."

One by one the pizza boxes emptied as plates filled with slices and generous helpings of salad. Bottle after bottle appeared from Yvonne's parents' wine cellar until a small army of glasses grew in the center of the table. Tinsley sated her hunger with a plain slice and forkfuls of Caesar salad, sipping at the merlot someone had set in front of her, the fruity wine bringing her taste buds alive. She felt ravenous. Who knew how many calories sledding could burn? Or maybe it was stewing about what a giant fake Sleigh was that had exhausted her.

She sawed through her piece of cheese pizza with a knife and fork from the same silver set her parents owned. A twinge of sadness shot through her as she realized how much she wished she were gathered around her *own* family dining room table instead of camped out in Yvonne's apartment with Sleigh Monroe-Hill.

Yvonne clinked her fork against the glass, her pale blue eyes shining in the candlelight. "Everyone has to go around and say what they're thankful for." Tinsley felt a tiny bit sorry for Yvonne, knowing that come Monday most of the Owls in her apartment would treat her with the same disregard they had previous to her Thanksgiving blowout. No one was about to start inviting her to *their* parties. Herself included. "I'll start," Yvonne continued. "I'm thankful to be able to share this weekend with everyone."

"Aww," Jeremy said as he came in to swipe more pizza. "Isn't that precious?" He gave Tinsley a lascivious smile, which she politely ignored. He'd been hitting on her all day.

"Shut up, *Jerm*." Yvonne sneered.

"I'm thankful the Lions are up a touchdown." Jeremy stuck a bottle of wine under his arm and made off with half a cheese pizza.

"I'm thankful he's not *my* brother," Rifat, on Yvonne's left, joked.

Fueled by the wine and the free food, the thanks-fest went around the table, and Tinsley suffered through tributes to world peace, animal rights, and the new album from Five Times Fast before someone said, "I'm just thankful for a weekend away from Waverly." A cheer of "hear, hear!" went around the table, everyone lifting their glasses. Tinsley clinked glasses with Julian, whose gold-flecked brown eyes caught her own for a split second before he took a swallow of wine.

That, Tinsley wanted to shout gleefully. *That look is why I will never concede to Sleigh Monroe-Hill.*

"What about you, Sleigh?" Yvonne asked. "You haven't said anything." How did they even know each other in the first place? At Waverly, Sleigh had been the worst kind of snob, and now she was buddy-buddy with Yvonne? Weird.

"I know." Sleigh gazed toward the ceiling, her pale eyes taking on a dreamy look that either came from Yvonne's brother's pot or her own ethereal sense of well-being. "It's just that there's so much to be thankful for." She paused dramatically and a hush fell over the dining room. Tinsley wanted to puke on every single one of Sleigh's round brown freckles. One of the votive candles burned out and a hand reached out of the darkness and silently relit it. "I'm thankful for WILDFAM, the organization that sent me to the Dominican Republic to work on houses," she finally said. "It changed my entire outlook on life."

Tinsley put her head down and rolled her eyes. Christ, not the poor homeless Dominicans again. Didn't she have any other shtick?

"I'm thankful for people who care about other people," Julian said suddenly, glancing at Sleigh. Tinsley took a gulp of wine to recover. What did he mean by that? Was that directed at Sleigh? He wasn't seriously interested in her, was he? First Julian dumped her for Jenny Humphrey, and now he was ditching her again for evil incarnate Sleigh Monroe-Hill? Sleigh wasn't nicer than her—Sleigh wasn't nicer than *anybody*. The thought sickened her, and before she could stop it, the words came tumbling out of her mouth.

"I'm thankful for a roommate who doesn't throw my shit out the window," she said sweetly, the wine buzzing in her head.

Even in the low light, Tinsley could see Sleigh turn bright red. Immediately, her shining, happy face cracked. "You fucking deserved it!" she shouted, a blue vein in her eyelid pulsing to life. She pushed away from the table, her tomato sauce–covered fork clattering on the floor in her wake. Tinsley watched her go, biting her lip to keep a smug smile from forming on her face.

Giggles broke out around the table. "I totally remember seeing all your shoes sprawled out across the lawn!" Rifat Jones spoke up, shaking her head. "I didn't realize that was the same Sleigh."

Tinsley just smiled and let everyone talk, grateful that the psycho's secret was finally out.

Julian turned to Tinsley. "I guess it was too much to hope for."

"What? A nice roommate?" Tinsley asked in surprise. She could feel the others staring at them.

"Sleigh told me all about what happened freshman year," Julian said. "She said you constantly provoked her until she just cracked." His eyes scanned Tinsley's face, and she suddenly felt like she was naked—and not sexy-naked, but nightmare, in-the-middle-of-class naked. "She regrets what she did. She says she's a better person now, and I believe her. She's changed, but you clearly haven't." He stood up from the table, carefully placing his crumpled napkin on his plate, and disappeared into the living room.

"Speaking of roommates," Jenny cried out, causing everyone, transfixed by the drama, to turn toward her. "I'm totally thankful to not be having dinner with my father and all the Hare Krishnas bunking at my house right now!"

Everyone laughed, and Jenny explained how the three of them had walked into an apartment full of orange robes and bald heads—and a live turkey. Other people started to tell stories of nightmare holidays, and the clink of forks against china resounded once again through the dining room.

Tinsley sat silent, her insides quaking. Why did she have to say that? Sleigh totally deserved it . . . but still. The thought of Julian rushing away to comfort Sleigh made her sick, and she kept visualizing him brushing her messy blond hair out of her face and kissing the tears off her cheeks.

"You okay?" Jenny whispered, nudging Tinsley's waist.

Tinsley smiled wistfully and looked into Jenny's concerned face. "I'm thankful we don't hate each other anymore," she whispered.

Jenny smiled back. "Me too."

If only Tinsley could have as much luck winning Julian over.

21

A WAVERLY OWL DOES NOT ENGAGE IN ILLEGAL
DRINKING—UNLESS IT IS SANCTIONED BY A
FACULTY MEMBER.

Brandon took another swig of kirsch, the sweet cherry taste burning the back of his throat. The alcohol—they'd been drinking throughout the afternoon, from the first course of lauded German sausage to the last course of recently slaughtered turkey—made his head buzz and he closed his eyes, resting momentarily. What with the murdering of a defenseless bird, the repeated rounds of Dutch Blitz, and an extended sauna with his roommate and their old German teacher, suffice it to say that Thanksgiving had been surreal this year. Maybe not the worst Brandon ever had—he remembered being stuck in the Newark airport for eighteen hours once, on his family's way to Bermuda, his cranky, pregnant stepmother shoveling Hostess cupcakes into her mouth like she was a refugee—but close. After a whole day trapped inside Mr. Dunderdorf's house, Brandon was feeling claustrophobic and jittery, ready to dash out the door and run all the way back to campus whenever the opportunity presented itself.

But Heath refused to let him. "Dude," he kept whispering, "don't be so gay." Brandon couldn't help it—he could only be called gay so many times in two days before he had to prove he wasn't. And so Brandon let himself be convinced the twins were worth it, if only so that he wouldn't have to trudge back to his dorm room and sit alone in the darkness, thinking about Sage.

"Dude," Heath said, for like the ten thousandth time that day. "This stuff is, like, grain alcohol." Heath let out what could only be described as a giggle as he tipped his glass back. He licked his lips, his eyes glazing over slightly.

"Here we are." Mr. Dunderdorf thundered back into the front room with a family photo album tucked under each arm. Brandon wished he could've begged off, as Mrs. Dunderdorf had hours ago—she said she needed to take care of some things in the kitchen, but when Brandon went to the bathroom, he spied her sitting on a kitchen stool watching a soap opera on a tiny TV. "Nothing like starting at the very beginning. This is the house I grew up in." Mr. Dunderdorf pointed at a faded black-and-white photograph of a small, Alpine lodge, four men in lederhosen and two angry-looking goats standing sternly in front of it. Brandon wanted to kill himself.

"Do you have any more cherry water?" Heath asked innocently, holding up the glass he'd emptied for the fifth time. "It's just so delicious."

Mr. Dunderdorf's eyes twinkled. "You've got a taste for kirsch, eh? Excellent." He strained to hoist himself up from the couch, and Brandon was grateful for the chance to get the old man's lederhosen out of his sight. "Let's see." He disappeared into the kitchen.

Heath stretched out his legs and closed his eyes. "What time did he say the twins were getting in?"

Brandon searched his memory, but his brain was fuzzy. "Late." His stomach rumbled. He knew it made him look like a pussy, but he hadn't been able to eat any of the turkey Mrs. Dunderdorf sliced onto his plate without thinking of the poor animal scurrying around the backyard. Maybe he should work for PETA and hook up with some of those hippie animal-rights girls. Then he remembered his brief, ill-fated tryst with "I don't see anyone exclusively" Elizabeth from St. Lucius, and realized he'd already tried that.

"Christ, I wish they'd just get here already," Heath mumbled. He licked his lips again. "I'm already shitfaced."

"Yeah, me too," Brandon seconded. He avoided looking at the cuckoo clock as it chimed the hour—Brandon couldn't even keep track of the dongs, and couldn't bear to glance at his cell phone. "Hey, what are their names, do you remember?"

Heath sat bolt upright. "Shit, I don't know. Everyone just calls them the Dunderdorf twins." He pressed his fingers to his temples, trying to channel all the gossip of years gone by for a mention of the twins' first names. "Dammit."

Mr. Dunderdorf reappeared with a fresh bottle of kirsch, and Brandon drained the last few gulps in his glass before holding it out for a refill. Mr. Dunderdorf filled both their glasses, but only halfway. "We should pace ourselves, gentlemen, no? I'm sure you're not used to drinking." He nudged past Brandon and retook his seat between them, spreading the photo album out on his wide lap.

"This is a shot of me on the Waverly lawn when I arrived for my first year of teaching." Mr. Dunderdorf turned a page with his wrinkled hands. The whole house smelled like German sausage.

"Who's that?" Brandon asked, pointing at the young man standing next to Dunderdorf.

"That's your very own Dean Marymount," Mr. Dunderdorf replied. "He was one of my most promising young German students."

"No way." Heath leaned forward. "He had hair."

"Oh, yes." Mr. Dunderdorf nodded. "He was quite the ladies' man." The professor took a long drink of kirsch.

"Really?" Brandon asked, sensing that Dunderdorf was something of a gossip. Maybe they could at least get some juicy stories out of their long, wasted day.

Dunderdorf snorted. "He was known to have a few faculty dalliances in his day." He rubbed his chin, covered in white stubble. "Not that I know much about that."

"Like with who?" Heath wanted to know. Brandon knew it was a major goal of Heath's to have sex with some hot young teacher before graduating—but the best he'd managed to get so far was a pat on the head from Mrs. Seraphim, the chemistry teacher.

Mr. Dunderdorf shook his head. "It's not for me to say," he answered, to their disappointment. "I doubt you would know any of them anyway." He flipped the page as a way of putting an end to the conversation. "Ah, our trip to EuroDisney," he sighed.

Heath leaned in. "Are those your daughters?" Brandon leaned in too. The photo was of Mr. and Mrs. Dunderdorf and two blond six-year-old girls dressed in matching Minnie Mouse costumes.

"Yes," Mr. Dunderdorf said. He sighed. "All these years. It seems like only yesterday they were this small. You'll see when you meet them."

"I can't wait," Heath said anxiously.

"What are their names?" Brandon asked.

Mr. Dunderdorf pointed at the matching Minnies. "This is Helga, and this is Gretchen."

Heath made a face behind Mr. Dunderdorf's back, as if to say, *They'd better not be as ugly as their names.*

"You'll see when you become fathers yourselves," Mr. Dunderdorf told them, wistfully. For a second his eyes got watery, and Brandon hoped he wasn't about to cry. Instead he sneezed, then blew his nose on the faded handkerchief stuffed in his shirt pocket. "It all goes by too fast."

Mr. Dunderdorf flipped over a few pages in the photo album, fast-forwarding the years. "Here's a more recent picture," he said. "My lovely girls."

Heath choked on his kirsch, coughing into his hand. Brandon leaned in to see the picture of two gangly blondes in lederhosen, both flashing sets of braces complete with attached headgear. One of the twins had some kind of ultra-kinky perm, her blond hair in tiny corkscrews, while the other had a polka-dotted turquoise headband and leather half-boots that looked like they belonged on *Miami Vice*.

Brandon shot Heath a glare. Hot girls? Delicious Swiss Misses? More like metal-mouthed ugly ducklings with zero fashion sense and what looked like terrible cases of acne. The whole stupid day had come down to this—what a nightmare. How the hell was he supposed to make Sage jealous by making out with a girl who looked like she had a recycling center in her mouth?

Heath pretended not to notice Brandon's look, instead asking Mr. Dunderdorf if kirsch was the national beverage of Germany—because if it wasn't, it certainly should be. Pleased by his students' interest in German culture, Dunderdorf refilled their glasses once again.

The next three photo albums were a blur of boring stories, terrible pictures, and poses of the unattractive twins in just about every city in Eastern Europe. Brandon felt his own eye-lids staying closed longer between blinks.

"You boys are tired," Mr. Dunderdorf announced, slamming the photo album shut.

"Yes!" Brandon said, suddenly awake. At last. They could stumble back home, pass out, and erase this entire day—maybe starting with last night, when Sage dumped him—from his memory. Brandon's legs wobbled and he caught himself on the arm of the couch.

"Upstairs." Mr. Dunderdorf pointed. "You can sleep it off in the spare bedroom. No sense in going back to campus. That could be bad for both of us, no?" He shook the empty bottle of kirsch mischievously.

"Oh, we couldn't impose," Brandon protested, but even as he said it he wondered if he'd even be able to make it back to the dorms. His forehead was sweating, and suddenly, drinking all that kirsch no longer seemed like a great idea.

"I insist." Somehow, Heath and Brandon reluctantly agreed— at this point, they were totally defeated. As they followed Dunderdorf up the musty carpeted stairs that reminded Brandon of his grandmother's dilapidated Victorian in Danbury, Connecticut, Brandon's legs felt heavy and wooden. Dunderdorf led them to a spare room with two twin beds pushed under the pitched ceiling. The rest of the space was crammed with boxes marked alternately with the names HELGA and GRETCHEN. As a testament to how exhausted they were, Heath and Brandon sank into their respective beds without investigating the treasure trove—in normal spirits, Heath wouldn't have rested until he found some satin panties and put them under his pillow.

"How did I let you talk me into this?" Brandon asked drunkenly. "I thought they were supposed to look like Heidi Klum."

Heath moaned before rolling over and kicking the covers onto the floor. Brandon stared up at the slanted ceiling, his mouth dry, his brain haunted by the image of Sage's beautiful face laughing at him.

OwlNet   Instant Message Inbox

EmilyJenkins: U just missed it—TC just slapped down Sleigh MH.

BennyCunningham: AFT. That girl's a BEEYOTCH. Any bloodshed?

EmilyJenkins: Not yet. But I think it has something to do w/ JULIAN.

BennyCunningham: Not surprising it's about a boy again—even a frosh.

EmilyJenkins: Dunno . . . TC ended up looking bad. . . . Maybe SMH finally can get back at her.

BennyCunningham: My money's on Tinsley. Every time.

EmilyJenkins: What if Sleigh comes back to Waverly?

BennyCunningham: She's not sharing my room!

A WAVERLY OWL KNOWS HOW TO HAVE A GOOD TIME IN ANY SITUATION—JUST NOT *TOO* GOOD A TIME.

Callie hoisted herself onto a red leather stool at the granite kitchen counter and stuck her thumb in the almost empty glass pan of brownies sitting on top of the stainless steel stove. She licked off the crumbs, wishing someone had thought to save her a whole brownie. (Although, with Yvonne's brother and his friends, who knew what they were laced with.) Parched from the day's activities, she raised her wineglass and took a huge swallow.

Ellis tossed his hooded parka on a kitchen stool and fanned through the stack of pizza boxes piled on the counters, looking for any leftovers. "Man, you're a half an hour late for dinner and it's all gone."

Callie laughed, kicking off her soaked socks. She wasn't used to hanging out with guys just as friends. There was something completely refreshing about it, and she hadn't laughed so much in one day in a long, long time. After they'd creamed the two ten-year-olds in a snowball fight, they'd crossed into Brooklyn and strolled through Park Slope, peeking through the windows of all the closed boutiques. They'd stopped for scallion pancakes at a Chinese place that was open, but even so, Callie was starved by the time they made it back to the Upper East Side.

Yvonne's kitchen—and entire apartment—was in a state of total, post-Thanksgiving-pizza-dinner disarray, and Callie could hear the noise of the sliding glass doors opening and closing as people plunged into the hot tub.

Except, no sign of Tinsley or Jenny. The idea that they were off together doing something more fun seemed impossible. But for once Callie didn't drive herself crazy thinking about it.

"Want a drink?" Ellis grabbed a bottle of merlot from the stainless steel wine rack in the pantry and swiftly opened it with a rabbit-shaped opener. He poured himself a full glass of wine and swirled it around in the glass like an expert.

"Yes, please. My mom always drinks merlot," Callie said randomly, thinking about her mother, and how angry she'd been when Callie had called last night to say she wasn't coming home. Callie slid a thick, strawberry blond lock behind her still cold ear. She watched as he filled another glass. "Not that she drinks all that often. She's a governor and really boring. What does your mom do?"

Ellis sipped his wine. "She's an artist."

"Really?" Callie asked, leaning her elbows on the counter. That was much cooler than her mom's job. Ellis had probably never been forced to attend a state dinner wearing a pair of white gloves. "Like, what kind of art?"

"She mostly does collages with found objects—you know, stuff she comes across on the street, in the subway, et cetera." Ellis ran a hand through his hair and shrugged.

"Like trash?" Callie had a brief vision of a well-dressed Upper East Side woman plucking a dirty tissue from a gutter and sticking it to a piece of canvas. Ew.

Ellis laughed, and Callie caught a glimpse of a silver filling in the back of his mouth. "She prefers to call it 'recycled memories.' Sometimes it's trash, but mostly it's things like letters or postcards or, I don't know, buttons."

"It sounds cool," Callie admitted, thinking how much her mother would hate having a collage of buttons and gum wrappers hanging in their dining room. "I'd like to see it sometime."

"Yeah?" Ellis looked surprised. "I'll have to take you to her studio, then. She's got this great space down off Broome Street."

"That would be fun," Callie said, meaning it. She watched as Ellis poured her another glass of wine, then set the bottle back on the counter. A tiny splotch of pizza sauce had landed on the neck of his shirt.

"What?" he asked, noticing Callie's eyes on him. "Did I spill wine all over myself?" He glanced down at his shirt.

"No." Callie pushed off the stool, the tile floor cold on her bare feet. "Pizza." She grabbed a crumpled linen napkin and ran water over the edge of it, then stepped toward Ellis. Her hand shook almost imperceptibly as she dabbed the napkin against the pizza sauce, her mind whirling. She felt his eyes on her face, and it seemed like he was closer than two inches away from her.

And then she noticed that her ring was gone.

She let out a shriek and pushed away from Ellis, her eyes searching the dark tiled floor for any flash of her amethyst ring.

"What is it?" Ellis asked, a tone of concern in his voice.

"I lost it," Callie moaned, completely panicked. Her fingers plowed through pizza crusts and bits of dried toppings, but no ring.

"What?" Ellis asked patiently. He came around to her side of the table and dropped to one knee.

"My ring." She put her head in her hands, pressing her fingertips to her forehead, trying to remember when she'd last seen it. Had she taken it off at any point during the day? "My gloves!" She sprang to her feet, but a check of her gloves didn't turn up the promise ring.

"Where could it be?" Ellis asked helpfully. "Did you look in your purse and your coat pocket?"

Callie did as Ellis suggested, but nothing. Then she remembered. Their snowball fight on the bridge. She'd taken off her gloves to shake off the wet snow clinging to them after she packed an ice-ball extra tight. Her ring must have come off with it.

"The snowball fight." Callie felt her bottom lip quivering. She wasn't going to cry in front of Ellis. Her shoulders sagged in defeat. "I shook out my gloves. It's lost."

Ellis touched her back, a half-hug, half-pat. "I'm sure he'll understand," he said tenderly. "Just explain what happened. It was an accident."

"Oh my God!" Callie exclaimed. "What time is it?"

Ellis looked at the digital green numbers on the microwave, which Callie hadn't even noticed until just now. "It's eight," he answered.

Callie's head cleared, the wine buzz suddenly gone when she thought of a bewildered Easy, probably in military fatigues, alone on top of the Empire State Building. Waiting for her. She bolted for the door, throwing on her coat and gloves in one quick movement. "I'm late."

Ellis threw on his coat. "I'll get the cab for you." She stabbed the elevator button repeatedly with her thumb. All she could think about was the boy on top of the tallest building in New York, wondering where the hell his girlfriend was.

A WAVERLY OWL STANDS UP FOR HERSELF.

Brett helped her mother put the last of the Thanksgiving dinner dishes into the dishwasher, even offering to help her father dry the pots and pans as he bent over the sink, his shirtsleeves rolled up to the elbow. She'd been feeling protective of her parents since the alien Coopers had washed up on their shores, and she was finally, for maybe the first time in her life, beginning to truly appreciate Becki and Stuart Messerschmidt.

And as excruciating as any sit-down with the Coopers could be, Thanksgiving dinner hadn't been so bad. First, Sebastian had had a ten-minute conversation with her father about how TiVo could be the greatest invention of the twenty-first century. And when Mrs. Cooper had gasped when her mother unveiled the yams with a top layer of burnt marshmallows, just like Brett liked them, Sebastian had said, "You rock, Mrs. Messerschmidt."

All in all, her plan had worked perfectly. Right after a Brett-initiated discussion on which celebrity had the worst breast implants (Brett's parents voted for Pamela Anderson, while Sebastian picked out Posh Spice), and right before the pumpkin pie was passed around, Mr. Cooper announced that he and his wife would be heading back to Greenwich after the meal, instead of staying another night. Mrs. Cooper tried to smooth things over by blaming it on the weather forecast for the next day, but Brett couldn't help beaming triumphantly.

Brett tucked the leftovers into the overstuffed refrigerator. "Turkey sandwiches all weekend," her father smiled, rubbing his belly.

"Should I toss the buns?" her mother asked.

"Leave them out," her father said. "Someone might want to nosh later."

Brett balanced the Tupperware container of sugar on top the flour container and carried them into the walk-in pantry. Peaches, one of her mother's dogs, bolted between her legs and the sugar container shook precariously.

"What do you think you're doing?"

Brett turned around slowly. Her sister slammed the pantry door behind her. She was red-faced, her hands on her hips.

"Helping in the kitchen while you guys have aperitifs." The pantry smelled like cinnamon and apples, and the shelves were crammed with everything from jars of her mother's favorite black olives to giant Tupperware containers of Christmas cookie cutters.

"You know what I mean!" Bree turned a shade of purple Brett had never seen before. It wasn't a good look for her, but neither was the head-to-toe Ann Taylor outfit. "Since when do you wear those clothes?" Bree demanded. She reached out to touch the sleeveless Bon Jovi shirt—another eighth-grade relic—Brett had changed into after spilling gravy on her other shirt.

"Since when do you wear *those* clothes?" Brett reached to finger Bree's rose-print dress. "You look like a choir girl."

Bree pressed her lips together until they almost turned white. The last time Brett had seen her that angry, she'd just found out that Melanie Spiegelman had bought the same dress for the senior prom. "And who *is* that guy? I'll bet he doesn't even go to Waverly. You picked him up at the train station and invited him into our home. Admit it."

"When did you become such a goddamn snob?" Brett's blood boiled, but she kept her voice low. "Even if I did, it would still be better than what *you* brought into our house. I'd rather have Thanksgiving in a goddamn soup kitchen than spend another minute with those people. They totally have sticks up their asses. And you do too if you can't see it. Why are you trying so hard to pretend you're one of them?"

"At least I'm not consorting with drug dealers," her sister shot back.

Brett wanted to reach out and smack her sister. She and Bree had always been close, which meant they'd had their fair share of catfights and screaming matches. But never before had Bree seemed so alien. Brett wanted to take the Tupperware container of flour and throw it all over Bree's perfect outfit. Instead, she set it down cautiously on one of the pantry shelves and crossed her arms smugly over her chest. "I *knew* it would work."

"Knew *what* would work?" Bree asked.

"The only reason I invited Sebastian over was to scare you and your future monsters-in-law off." She fought the urge to stick out her tongue. "And guess what? It worked."

Brett pushed past Bree to escape the suddenly stifling pantry and froze when she saw the Coopers and Sebastian standing with her parents in the kitchen. The Coopers pretended to admire the granite countertop while Brett's mother crossed her arms, looking at her with disappointment. Sebastian's chain wallet jingled as he shoved his hands into his pockets, his shoulders sagging.

"We were just getting ready to leave," Mr. Cooper spoke up, addressing Brett's parents as if they hadn't just heard Brett say they had goddamn sticks up their asses. "Thank you for an . . . interesting day." They marched out of the kitchen, Bree, Willy, and Brett's parents on their heels.

Alone with Sebastian, Brett wanted to say she was sorry for all the drama. But her pulse was still racing from the fight with Bree and her mind was totally blank. What she wanted right now was to sneak a couple of her dad's beers into the family room, collapse into the giant squishy couch, and pop in *Spider-Man*. Maybe curl up under one of her mom's fleecy leopard-print throws. "Do you want to—" she started to ask, but Sebastian cut her off.

"I guess it's time for me to go too." He had a funny look on his face.

"Oh." Brett tilted her head to the side, surprisingly disappointed. "Please don't—" But before she could finish, he'd already left.

 **Owl**Net

From: BrettMesserschmidt@waverly.edu

To: CallieVernon@waverly.edu; JennyHumphrey@waverly.edu;

Date: KaraWhalen@waverly.edu

Subject: Thursday, November 28, 8:15 P.M.
Thanksgiving Day bust

Recipe for a shitty T-Day:

Take a bunch of pretentious future in-laws without souls, mix in a suddenly vapid sister and completely docile parents, add a cranky Jersey boy for a twist and—bam! Watch it explode.

Sigh. Hope you girls had more fun than I did. Tell me funny stories to cheer me up, please, since I'm stuck in NJ and the malls don't open until 9 A.M. Can't wait to be back at school.

Xo

B

A WAVERLY OWL DOESN'T PROFESS HER LOVE—
AT LEAST NOT UNTIL THE SECOND DATE.

"It's freezing out here!" Jenny squealed as she stepped out onto the rooftop terrace, a thick white Egyptian cotton towel wrapped around her black Calvin Klein tank and matching boy-shorts. She shuffled toward the hot tub, her toes stuffed into someone's shoes to make it across the slushy deck. Tinsley, Kara, Yvonne, and half a dozen others were already crowded into the steaming hot tub, but Kara and Casey moved apart to make a spot for Jenny.

"Just jump in," Casey said, a devilish grin on his face. "You'll feel much better."

How could she *not* be falling in love with this guy? He was just so . . . tempting. After their perfect kiss that morning, they'd spent the whole day together—skating at Rockefeller Center, which Jenny hadn't done in years, having a snowball fight on Madison Avenue in front of all the fancy boutiques, sipping hot chocolate in some hole-in-the-wall diner.

But one glance at Tinsley reminded her that she was supposed to be *just having fun*. She grabbed a wine cooler and stuck a toe in the hot water. Then she dropped her towel and quickly sank into the water just low enough so that her oversize chest was submerged. Her head was light from a game of quarters—otherwise, she might not have had the courage to hop into the hot tub, at least not with Tinsley there, her toned body perfect in her matching pink Ralph Lauren bra-and-panty set. Jenny closed her eyes and counted slowly to three before taking a sip of the wine cooler, the cold, fruity elixir tickling her tongue. Tinsley had told her to just have fun, and she was doing just that. Starting with, oh, six drinks or so over the course of the evening.

"Isn't this crazy?" Kara Whalen spoke up, her pale brown hair wet and clinging to her bare shoulders. "Being in a hot tub in Manhattan in the middle of a snowstorm?"

"Is there room for another body in here?" Julian McCafferty stepped through the glass doors and scooped a handful of snow from a potted plant. He dropped his towel, revealing his thin but muscular torso and a pair of Hawaiian-print Gap boxers with strawberries all over them. Jenny and Tinsley exchanged a glance—it was obvious that Julian wasn't looking at Tinsley, after he'd chastised her in the dining room.

"There is for yours!" Yvonne Stidder giggled and took another sip of her wine cooler. Her blond hair was pulled into a frizzy ponytail and her glasses were completely fogged over. They'd been playing drinking games since dinner, and now everyone was pleasantly toasted. Yvonne scooted over toward Tinsley, leaving a big space next to her that Julian sank into.

"Whatcha all doing out here?" Julian slipped further into the hot water until just his head was visible. Jenny leaned back, staring at the dark night sky and letting the water bubble up around her ears. She thought she could feel Casey's knee bump against hers underwater.

"How much is there to do in a hot tub?" Yvonne stumbled over her words as she slid closer to Julian. She adjusted the strap of her yellow C&C tank, a color that made her look like one of those marshmallow Easter chicks.

"How 'bout a nice little game of Truth or Dare?" Casey spoke up, taking another swig from his beer. His dark curls were damp and plastered across his forehead. When he'd tugged off his T-shirt, Jenny had almost fainted. He had a gorgeous swimmer's body—muscular shoulders tapering to a slender, toned abdomen. "You don't get to play it as much in college."

"How come?" Jenny asked, sinking down so that her shoulders went under the wonderfully hot water. Her head felt deliciously fuzzy, and it was all she could do not to throw her arms around Casey and start kissing him in front of everyone. He was just so *cute*.

Casey leaned toward her and raised his eyebrows. She felt his breath on her skin. "We play much more *sophisticated* games," he said jokingly. She wouldn't have minded learning what they were.

"All right—Tinsley. Truth or dare?" Clifford Montgomery, the water polo player at Waverly who was completely in love with Tinsley, leaned toward her.

"Dare," Tinsley said boredly as she reached up and twisted her wet hair into a bun at the nape of her neck. She'd been surprised to see Julian come out to the hot tub at all—or at least without stupid Sleigh Monroe-Hill—since he'd been completely reluctant even to be in the same room with Tinsley since dinner. Where was Sleigh, anyway? Maybe she'd gone home, satisfied now that she'd completely ruined Tinsley's chances with Julian forever.

"I dare you to kiss Kara." Cliff grinned from ear to ear.

"Hey!" Kara protested. "It wasn't my dare." She crossed her arms over her chest. "Just because I've kissed girls in the past . . ."

Rolling her eyes, Tinsley stood up in the hot tub and quickly leaned over to Kara, kissing her softly on her cheek, right near her lips. "Sorry," Tinsley whispered before sinking back to her own spot in the tub and staring up at the cloudy sky.

"No fair." Cliff waved his empty beer bottle around in the air. "There was no tongue."

Casey pointed a finger at him. "Guess next time you'll know to specify, dude." He laughed and leaned back, casually throwing his arm around Jenny's bare shoulders. It felt heavenly. The stark night air was cool against her hot skin, and she felt each snowflake as it landed on her and melted. Beneath the water, she could feel Casey's foot lightly touch hers. Everything just felt . . . perfect.

This was the Best. Thanksgiving. Ever.

"Truth or dare, Jenny?" Tinsley flicked a finger against the surface of the water, sending a tiny spray in Jenny's direction.

Not wanting to have to kiss any girls, Jenny opted for truth.

Casey spoke up before Tinsley could say anything. "So, Jenny, if you had to kiss anyone in this hot tub, who would it be?" he demanded in a hushed voice.

Jenny giggled. He was so cute. Her wine cooler–soaked brain managed to tell her mouth to say what she'd actually been thinking, which was, "You, silly! You know I love you!"

Giggles broke out, but before Jenny could open her mouth to say anything more, Tinsley was practically on top of her, reaching a hand under Jenny's arm and tugging her to her feet.

"You're coming with me." Tinsley pushed Jenny out of the tub and threw a crumpled towel around her shoulders.

"But I don't want to go anywhere!" Jenny wailed, turning back to the hot tub and drunkenly waving at everyone. The group cheered back at her.

Jenny dropped the towel from her shoulders, and Tinsley had the feeling that if she didn't get Jenny out right now, the next thing she'd be dropping—now that the *L* word was already out there—would be her clothes. "Let go!"

"You are drunk," Tinsley hissed. She squeezed Jenny's forearm harder, grabbed her towel off the ground, and shoved her through the sliding glass doors.

At the sight of two scantily clad, dripping wet girls, the living room, filled with clouds of marijuana smoke and college boys playing video games, erupted into appreciative hoots.

"Come hang out with us!" Jeremy Stidder called as Tinsley pushed Jenny down the hallway toward the bathroom. Once inside, the door locked behind them, Tinsley poured Jenny a giant plastic cup of water.

"What are we doing in here?" Jenny turned the knob but couldn't figure out the lock. Her head lolled around like it was too heavy for her neck to support, and her eyes were completely glazed over. "I want to be out there . . . with Casey."

"Drink." Tinsley handed the glass to Jenny, who obediently sipped it down. She flicked a switch on the wall and a red heat lamp overhead whirred to life.

"Uh-oh." Jenny abruptly set the cup down on the bathroom counter. In her loose white towel and with her dark hair plastered to her head, she looked like a kid. And in a way, she really kind of was one. All the more reason she shouldn't be professing her love to guys she didn't even know.

"What's the matter?" Tinsley asked warily, shivering a little. She'd caught a glimpse of Julian as she forced Jenny out of the tub. From the look on his face, she knew the scene was just further evidence of what a bossy bitch Tinsley Carmichael was.

"I think I'm gonna . . ." Jenny trailed off, but Tinsley recognized the greenish cast to her skin and quickly rushed Jenny
over to the toilet. She held her hair back as all of the wine
coolers Jenny had guzzled—as well as her efforts to remain
detached and just have fun—swirled down the drain.

25

A WAVERLY OWL DOESN'T JUDGE A GIRL BY HER
CLOTHING—ESPECIALLY IF SHE TAKES IT OFF.

The musty wood smell of the sauna filled Brandon's nose as he laid his towel along one of the benches. He wiped the sweat from his brow and stretched out across one of the cedar benches, adjusting his Ralph Lauren boxer briefs.

"This is beautiful." Heath stuffed his towel beneath his head and yawned. "Without Dunderdorf, I could get some serious relaxing done here."

After dinner they'd tossed and turned under the eaves of the stifling Dunderdorf twins' room, unable to fall asleep in such a strange setting. Brandon had originally balked at Heath's suggestion that they take a sauna to "sweat out their sexual frustration," but twenty sleepless minutes later, he had relented. Heath assured him he'd made the right choice, insisting that the sauna would "open Brandon's pores."

"I can feel the kirsch coming out of me." Heath closed his

eyes and took a giant gulp from one of the bottles of Evian they'd grabbed from the fridge on their way downstairs. "That stuff is foul."

"Evil," Brandon added, leaning his head back against the cedar wall and letting the steam help him sober up. He was still infinitely pissed at Heath for dragging him to Mr. Dunderdorf's under false pretenses—the fable about the supposedly legendary twins now seemed to him as fantastic as tales of the Loch Ness Monster, or Bigfoot—but he was happy, too, in a way. Happy to have something else to be miserable about besides Sage. The sting of Sage's sudden breakup had started to subside, if only because the whole day at the Dunderdorfs' had been so stifling and boring, it now felt like five years had gone by.

Steam filled the sauna and Brandon rubbed his tired eyes. Two faces at the glass sauna door startled him. "Heath!" he hissed, still slightly drunk.

A soft snore emanated from Heath.

"Heath." He snapped his towel at Heath, smacking him against his bare chest.

Heath opened one eye. "Huh?"

"Look. Over. There." Brandon indicated the sauna door just as it opened and Heath bolted upright. They watched in amazement as two girls armored in puffy ski jumpsuits—one orange, one blue—poked their heads in, their hair encased by thick wool caps. Their matching black-framed glasses fogged up immediately.

"Are you friends of our father's?" one of them asked, removing her glasses to clear the steam. A whoosh of cold air breezed into the sauna.

Brandon and Heath just stared, their mouths agape. Worse than the idea of the twins being phantoms was the actual sight of them in their dumpy clothes.

They're nerds, Brandon thought.

"We go to Waverly," Heath finally managed to say. He stuck his chest out a little—to him, even dorky girls were still girls. "Your father invited us over for Thanksgiving."

"Then you must have an opinion," the one in the blue said. "Is America really a democracy, or is it actually a republic?"

Heath's face, which had showed a glimmer of hope, immediately fell again. "No schoolwork on holidays," he grunted. Brandon was still too drunk to have any sort of political discussion, and wondered how they were going to get out of this. They couldn't be rude to Dunderdorf's kids, could they? But all Brandon wanted to do at this moment was grab his clothes and hightail it back to campus.

The other twin began unzipping her ski suit. "It's a democracy," she said, stepping out of the pants to reveal a pair of black leggings. "That's all Americans talk about. How they live in a democracy."

"I'm not stupid," her sister said, tossing her ski suit carelessly out the door, and pulling her cable-knit sweater covered in snowflakes over her head. "I know that. But it's not *really* a democracy." She shimmied out of her dark leggings, revealing a pair of long, slender legs. Brandon heard a gurgling sound from Heath as he watched in awe.

Brandon felt faint. It was like one of those dolls where there was another doll inside and the more dolls you found, the smaller the doll got—except this time, the dolls just kept getting *sexier*. The twins must've had twenty pounds of layering against the cold, which all ended up in a pile at the sauna door, their slim bodies, now in silky dove gray panties and matching bras, each with a tiny rose in the middle, looking nothing like the pictures of the girls in lederhosen. No braces, no dorky white boots, no terrible hairstyles. They'd grown up and matured—very, very nicely. Brandon looked at Heath, whose eyes were trained on the twins as they sauntered to the bench in the corner.

"Well?" the one nearest Brandon asked. Without her glasses, her gray-blue eyes, framed by dark lashes, were clear and sharp. They looked like some kind of gemstone, though Brandon, either from the kirsch or the steam or something else, couldn't remember which.

"It's definitely a democracy," Heath answered, sliding down the bench toward the girls.

The twins giggled. "See what I mean," one said to the other. Brandon couldn't stop staring at the sight of two beautiful, identical girls in matching bras and panties, tiny beads of sweat starting to form on their collarbones. He felt like he was in some kind of beer commercial, where the loser guy manages to score two hotties just because he's carrying the right kind of beer.

"I'm Helga, by the way," the twin sitting next to Brandon said. She slid the elastic off the end of one long braid and slowly untwined her hair. "And this is my sister, Gretchen."

Gretchen gave a short wave. "It's a republic, by the way." She flicked her braids over her shoulder. As she turned to smile at Heath, Brandon caught a glimpse of a tiny tattoo in the shape of a fairy on her shoulder blades. "Otherwise you wouldn't have the electoral college."

Heath shrugged, and Brandon could tell he had no idea what the electoral college was. "That's true," Brandon answered, learning forward, elbows on his knees. "What do they have in Switzerland?" Up close, the girls had skin that looked like white chocolate.

"They have everything." Brandon noticed that both girls slightly elided their *t*'s into *z*'s so that it sounded like she said, *Zey have everyzing*, which gave Brandon goose bumps. They could have been Bond girls. He watched as Helga opened a compartment in the sauna bench that neither he nor Heath had known existed and retrieved a pair of spray bottles. The girls squeezed the triggers, unleashing a cool mist around their heads and chests.

"How was the flight?" Brandon asked, shifting on the bench and trying not to think about how almost-naked these girls were. Heath, with a beatific smile on his face, seemed too dumbfounded to contribute.

"Fine." Helga leaned back against the bench. Or maybe it was Gretchen. No, Gretchen had the tattoo, right? "I read Goethe, and that always makes time fly." Brandon just nodded and tried not to stare at the tiny bead of sweat that was trickling down her chest.

"Where's your father?" Heath asked suddenly. His normally

relaxed face looked tense, like he was terrified Mr. Dunderdorf would run through the doorway at any moment, waving around his bloody turkey-killing ax and chasing them away.

"He's in a kirsch coma on the couch." Gretchen—or the one still in braids—touched Heath's arm casually, to calm him down. "He won't wake up until tomorrow."

"A kirsch coma on the couch," Helga repeated, and the girls erupted in laughter. There was something so incredibly sexy about the twins—besides the obvious killer bodies and gorgeous faces—that Brandon couldn't quite place. The way they played off each other, made jokes, asked questions, laughed big laughs. He tried to imagine Helga and Gretchen at Waverly. Who would they be friends with? He couldn't see Tinsley or Callie giving them the time of day, especially not if their puffy skiwear was any indicator of their fashion sense. Maybe Jenny. But Jenny liked everyone. He tried to imagine the twins on the Commons, laughing and arguing about politics, and then it occurred to him: The twins totally lacked self-consciousness. They had no idea how hot they were, because they didn't spend their whole life thinking about it, unlike most of the girls at Waverly.

"Maybe a little too much Thanksgiving fun for him." Heath perked up suddenly, now that he knew Dunderdorf was safely passed out. "Man, you're really lucky you missed out on killing the turkey."

"We're vegetarians." Gretchen spritzed herself again, the water droplets glistening on her skin.

"You really shouldn't eat animals." Helga collected her blond hair and magically twisted it up into one of those loose buns that girls with long hair were always making. "It's bad for the environment."

"So is having kids," Gretchen pointed out, poking her sister in her lean thigh. "And people don't seem to be stopping that."

"Heath has three already, so I guess he's not thinking about the environment." Brandon joked. The twins laughed.

"Whatever." Heath tossed his head, his sweaty hair plastered across his forehead. "My kids would totally kick your kids' asses, Buchanan." He took a swig from his bottle of water. "That's a guarantee."

But Brandon didn't hear much of the ensuing conversation. He was deep in thought about whether or not he should be in a sauna with the twins. Word was bound to get out via Heath's big mouth, and Sage had just broken up with him less than twenty-four hours earlier. Maybe she was at home right now, regretting what she'd said, ready to apologize come Monday morning. A rumor about a late-night sauna with the Swiss Misses would kill any chance he might have left with Sage Francis.

All he knew was he couldn't take his eyes of Helga . . . or Gretchen. "Can I borrow that?" he asked, holding out his hand for the spray bottle.

"Sure," Helga said, handing it to him.

Instead of spraying it on himself, though, he impulsively spritzed the water bottle directly at Helga and Gretchen, the mist landing on their perfectly trim vegetarian bellies. They threw their heads back with laughter and grabbed the bottle from his hands, spraying him back.

"So," Brandon said slyly, running a hand through his damp hair. "Your father asked us to spend the night. Sober up." He yawned. "I think I might head back up to that attic room he put us in."

Helga's pretty pink lips dropped open. "You can't sleep in there. It smells like . . . mothballs."

Gretchen's nose wrinkled as she wiped a bead of sweat off her collarbone. "And dead people."

"Well." Brandon took a deep breath and stared straight into Helga's baby blue eyes. "Is there anywhere else to sleep?"

Heath burst into a coughing fit as he took a sip from a bottle of water. Gretchen patted him grimly on the back.

Helga got to her feet and held out her hand to Brandon. "I'll show you my room."

Electricity surged through his body as he grabbed her hand and let her lead him out of the sauna.

"Shhh," Helga whispered as they made their way up the creaking basement stairs and through the dark living room. An empty bottle of kirsch sat on the coffee table. "They must be in bed." A strand of wet blond hair clung to her shoulder seductively.

Before he could stop himself, Brandon took a step forward and pressed his lips, gently but firmly, to the lock of hair on Helga's perfect, bare shoulder. She jumped slightly, and turned around. For one terrible second Brandon was sure she was going to start screaming in Switzerdeutsch and bring Dunderdorf down the stairs carrying a shotgun. But instead, she ran her hands up and down her arms and smiled shyly at Brandon. "That gave me goose bumps."

Heart thumping, Brandon stepped closer to her and let his lips brush lightly against her ear. He felt her body lean toward his, as though they were drawn together like magnets. "You smell amazing. Like wildflowers or something." And before he could think about how un-Brandon-like he was acting, his hands found Helga's hips and pulled her toward him.

"Are all you Waverly boys this forward?" she murmured softly. Outside the living room window, the moonlight shone against the smooth white snow.

"No," Brandon answered with a grin, his head suddenly clear. "You just got lucky." And he pressed his mouth to Helga's soft, waiting lips.

A WAVERLY OWL KNOWS WHEN TO KISS AND
MAKE UP.

Brett slammed the door to her bedroom, hard enough to shake the walls and send a thumbtack from the poster of Johnny Depp in *Pirates of the Caribbean* over her desk to the floor. She left it embedded in the rug, not caring if she stepped on it later, and threw her body down on her enormous bed. She was too pissed off at everyone to even appreciate how much softer and sweeter this mattress was than the creaky, worn-out twin bed in her dorm room. Her mind raced over what had happened—how could Bree corner her like that, or be so stupid to do it in a way that everyone could hear what they said? How dare she? What a giant bitch she'd become. Their whole fight was just so ugly and embarrassing—but *Bree* had made her act like that. It was totally, totally Bree's fault.

Brett pulled on her pair of comfy black DKNY pajama bot-

toms and checked her e-mail to see if Callie or Jenny had materialized yet . . . but nothing. Where *were* they? Probably having as crappy a Thanksgiving as she was. *I should just leave*, she
thought. Waverly had never seemed so appealing.

She touched her face and realized she was crying. She collapsed on her bed, surprised at how upset she was. The whole
plot to bust Bree and the Coopers had seemed like a good idea
when she conceived it—Sebastian had been so perfect. But the
hurt look he'd given her as he stalked out of their kitchen had
made her turkey-filled stomach ache. Brett lay back on her bed
and breathed deeply, trying to steady herself. Yes, she'd embarrassed Bree. And yes, it was Bree's fault . . . but maybe it was
hers, too. Even if the Coopers were totally lame, they were still
guests in Brett's house, and she could have been a little more
courteous. Or classy.

Shit. She could have pulled Bree aside—somewhere
private—and asked her why she was acting all brainwashed.
That would have been the mature thing to do.

She found Bree alone in the kitchen, pouring herself a glass
of water from the Brita pitcher. They hadn't really fought since
Bree went away to Columbia, and it felt really weird to know
she was actually angry with Brett.

"Hey," Brett said, her bare feet padding across the tile floor.

Bree looked up with a scowl on her pretty face—she was
still wearing her prissy dress, but at least she'd gotten rid of the
headband in her hair, and her auburn waves were falling mess-
ily around her face. "What do you want?"

"I want—" Brett's throat was dry. She wanted a drink of the

water in Bree's hand. She wanted a Thanksgiving weekend do-over. She wanted her sister back. "I want to say I'm sorry."

Bree looked at her skeptically, leaning against the counter.

"I'm sorry about the way I acted in front of Willy and his parents," Brett said, the words rushing out of her mouth. She stared out the dark window behind Bree's head, where she could see the reflection of the moon out on the water. "It was . . . childish."

"Well, I wish you could have realized that a little bit sooner." Bree plunked her cup down in the sink and started to leave the room. "The damage is done."

Brett reached out and touched Bree's bare arm. "I know, but I'm still sorry. I'll even apologize to the Coopers if you want me to." She suppressed a mild panic that Bree wasn't going to accept her apology. "But put yourself in my place. I come home from school and suddenly my house is filled with these totally stuck-up strangers, the house looks totally whitewashed, the dogs are locked in the laundry room, someone's forced my mother into khakis. . . ." Brett trailed off, watching her sister's face.

Bree pressed her lips together before she cracked a smile. "I had to take her to Talbots for those."

"She looked weird," Brett insisted. "I felt like I had to kind of make up for it with the Dolce & Gabbana skirt she got me for my birthday."

"It actually looked really good on you." Bree sighed. "Look, I'm sorry I tried to change everything here—but it's not because I'm ashamed of Mom and Dad. I just know how difficult Willy's parents are." Bree tapped her colorless nails against the counter and lowered her voice, although no one else was in the room. "But you don't get to pick your parents, or where you're from, or how you were brought up. And I really love Willy, so I'm willing to do whatever I have to do to make it work."

"He's totally hot, by the way." Brett opened the refrigerator and grabbed a Diet Coke. Cracking it open, she remembered how when she got to Waverly, she realized everyone in the world called it "soda" instead of "pop," and so she'd immediately started saying "soda," too, even though for her whole life she'd called it "pop." "Willy, I mean. Not Mr. Cooper."

"I know what you mean, goombah." Bree leaned over and tousled Brett's hair like she always did when she wanted to annoy her, but this time it felt really sweet. "Isn't he gorgeous? I mean, you should see him coming out of the shower when he's all dripping wet—"

"Too much information!" Brett squealed. "I definitely don't want to see that." Although she kind of did.

Bree shrugged, her green eyes finally happy again—just talking about Willy seemed to cheer her up. "So, I make an exception for Willy's parents because I love *him*. That's what love is about—taking the bad with the good. I don't expect you to do the same, but if you love me, maybe you will."

"I do." Brett nodded. "I love you."

"I love you too." Bree set the glass of water on the counter and threw her arms around Brett, who could feel the full force of Bree's body against her. She squeezed back, as hard as she could.

"Is Willy still here?" Brett asked, drying one of her eyes with a fingertip.

Bree nodded. "He's in the TV room with Dad."

"I'm really sorry I made his parents leave," Brett said, meaning it. Sort of. She was still kind of pleased with herself.

"I think we're all better off with them back in Greenwich." Bree smiled. "They haven't stayed away from their house in, like, twenty years. And then it was just to stay at the Yale Club in New York."

Brett laughed and followed Bree into the family room, where her parents were relaxing in matching La-Z-Boy recliners, watching some golf tournament in what looked like sunny Hawaii on the enormous plasma screen that took up half the wall.

"Hello, girls." Her father grinned a silly grin like he used to do when they were kids. "I see you've kissed and made up."

"For now." Bree poked Brett in the ribs, right where she was most ticklish. Both of them plopped down on the giant sofa, where Willy was sitting at one end. Brett folded her legs under her and leaned her head into the back of the cushions. The lamps gave off a soft glow and her father reached for the remote. He thumbed through the on-screen guide and found *Planes, Trains, and Automobiles*, a Messerschmidt family classic. He turned the volume up as Steve Martin and John Candy got drunk on airplane bottles of liquor and Brett felt her body release all its tension as the five of them turned their attention to the movie, grateful for a moment's peace. Her father began to snore quietly. Everything felt right with the world again.

Princess hopped up onto the couch, the tiny bell on her pink leopard-print collar jingling. As Brett stroked her soft fur, she remembered how cute it had been to see Sebastian, who liked to act all tough, with the tiny dog curled up on his lap. Brett felt a slightly queasy feeling in the pit of her stomach—but not wanting to admit that anything else was wrong, she blamed it on her second helping of mashed potatoes.

A WAVERLY OWL IS NEVER LATE FOR AN IMPORTANT ENGAGEMENT.

Callie peered out the windows of the yellow cab as it inched down Fifth Avenue, through the snowy darkness. Normally, she would have been thrilled to go in slow motion past Tiffany, watching the glamorous people stride in and out of the doors. But it was closed now, and all she cared about was getting to Easy as fast as humanly possible—something her cabdriver didn't seem to understand.

"Please!" Callie waved a twenty through the small window in the plastic divider. "Can you go any faster?"

"The snow, the snow," he kept saying.

The back of the cab was cold, but Callie didn't want to risk annoying the cabbie any further—it had taken ten minutes to even find one, and the snow was seeping through her boots. She rubbed her gloved hands up and down her legs, not believing she'd managed to lose track of time. What had she been thinking? She'd had all these plans to wear something gorgeous and sexy that would blow Easy away, but she hadn't even had time to put on more deodorant before zipping out of the apartment in the exact same outfit she'd been wearing all day.

Deep breaths, she told herself. *You'll get there.* It wasn't like Easy wasn't used to her being late. She stared at the gothic spires of St. Patrick's Cathedral, her mind drifting to her wedding day with Easy. Would they be married in a church like that? Maybe. And the Vera Wang dress would be perfect. Church bells tolled and they lurched forward, past the darkened windows of Saks Fifth Avenue reflecting a distorted image of the yellow cab.

Callie's stomach growled—the scallion pancakes in Brooklyn seemed like years ago. Her heart pounded and her whole body started to sweat. She definitely could have used some more deodorant. But as the yellow and blue–lit needle on top of the Empire State Building came into focus, she could sense Easy's presence. She was late, but she knew Easy would be waiting. As they pulled up next to it, Callie threw some bills at the driver and ran.

The heels of her Chloé boots clicked on the marble floor as she charged through the art deco lobby. Where the hell was she supposed to go? She strode toward the elevators.

"Whoa, whoa," a voice said. A guard dressed in blue and gray stepped out of the shadows of the elevator bank. "We're closing."

Callie noticed for the first time that the lobby was empty. "But it's not closing time." Callie pleaded. "I'm meeting someone." She took a step toward the open elevator, but the guard blocked her way.

"I'm sorry," he said, not sounding sorry at all. "But we're closing. It's Thanksgiving, and the weather's getting worse."

"But someone is *waiting* for me," Callie insisted. "He's already up there. I'm late and he's been waiting, don't you see?" Tears sprang to her eyes and threatened to spill over.

"I see," the guard assured her, gazing suspiciously at her. His hand rested on the black baton on his belt. "But I can't let you up. The building is closing." The guard touched his neatly trimmed moustache and checked his watch. "In fact, I'm supposed to lock up the central elevators now. You say someone is still up there?"

"Yes!" Callie said desperately. "The boy I love!" A few hot tears slid down her cheeks—she'd made it this far, and all that was standing between her and Easy now was a slightly pudgy security guard with some kind of God complex. "*Please.* I'm late already, and I'll . . . I'll scale the outside of this building if I have to." Callie's blood pulsed in her ears, and she was starting to feel nauseated at the thought of Easy wondering where the hell she was.

"Look, I can't—"

"You're married," she went on, catching the guard by surprise—she'd seen the gold band on his finger—"so you know what it's like to be totally in love with someone, right?" She raised her hand and flashed it in front of the guard's eyes to let him see her ring, but all her frozen hand revealed was a cold, white finger. "I already lost my promise ring—please don't let me lose him too."

The guard removed the green velvet rope in front of the open elevator. "Okay, but be quick. And then both of you get down here or you'll be stuck up there all night. I'm not kidding."

Callie planted a kiss on the guard's cheek before he knew what she was doing. "Thank you, thank you."

The elevator dinged shut and began to rise, shooting past the floors in the lower twenties and thirties, rocketing her toward the observation deck on the eighty-sixth floor. She remembered a trip to New York she'd taken with the junior high Model U.N. club her mother had forced her to join. Callie had been part of the International Court of Justice, the most boring part of Model U.N., and she'd threatened to quit, until her mother told her about the prize of a trip to New York City at the end of the school year. As the elevator rose through the upper floors, she remembered how one of her classmates had thrown up in the elevator. She felt like she might do the same just as the doors opened on the windy eighty-sixth floor, the cold winter air smacking her in the face.

A dark figure stepped forward from the edge of the observation deck. Callie recognized Easy's dark olive green Patagonia jacket, but his hair—his crazy-sexy, dark, almost-black curls—had been completely shorn off. He looked handsome—almost even more so—but different. His face caught the yellow light from the spire and she smiled. With his short hair, he looked like a schoolboy.

"Hey." The wind tousled the orange and red Hugo Boss scarf wound around his neck, her Christmas present to him last year. "I didn't think you were going to make it."

"Have you been waiting long?" she asked, annoyed at herself for asking such a mundane question. In the elevator she'd imagined jumping into Easy's arms, knocking them both to the ground, smothering him in kisses. But something about their whole scene at the top of the Empire State Building just felt . . . off.

"I had nowhere else to be." Easy grinned shyly, and Callie melted. She rushed toward him, letting him wrap his arms around her. She buried her face in his chest—even though there was still a knot in her stomach. It was so surreal to see him again after she'd been thinking about him for so long—it was almost like he wasn't the same person she'd been fantasizing about, even though, except for the hair, this was still the Easy Walsh she knew and loved.

Wasn't it?

Her gaze drifted off into the panoramic night view of New York, the dark rivers gurgling somewhere in the distance past the specks of bright lights. She babbled something about how she and Tinsley and Jenny couldn't find a hotel, how they'd ended up at Yvonne's, though she left out the part about the wild party, and spending the day with Ellis, and the magical trip through the underground world of art. She realized she was stalling, but she didn't know why.

"It's nice to just hear you talk again." Easy laughed, stroking her hair with his bare hands. He never wore gloves.

"Have you been painting?" she asked his chest.

He shook his head and took a step backwards. "They don't let you do that sort of thing." His beautiful blue eyes that always reminded her of stormy ocean waters looked a little harder than usual, and she shivered at the thought of Easy getting up at the crack of dawn to do push-ups. "I've been dreaming of you." He touched her chin and tenderly pulled her toward him for a kiss.

But Callie drew back.

"What?" Easy asked, confusion crossing his face. Snowflakes landed on his skin, melting away.

"I'm—it's—" Callie stammered, her heart feeling like it was about to explode. "Look." She tore off her gloves and held up her bare hand as tears spilled down her cheeks. "I lost your ring already. I'm so stupid. I was throwing snowballs and I—"

"It's okay." Easy tried to calm her down. He ran his hands up and down her back. "It's okay. It's just a ring."

"I know," Callie said bitterly. "But you gave it to me and I lost it." She realized then how stupid her bride fantasies were. She couldn't even stay committed to her fake engagement for a whole day. Guilt about how exactly she'd lost the ring—throwing snowballs with *Ellis*—made her fingers start to shake. But why did she feel guilty? She hadn't done anything *wrong*. And she knew she wasn't in love with Ellis—she hadn't even kissed him, or imagined kissing him. Before she'd met Ellis at Yvonne's, she'd touched Easy's ring every other minute, marveling at its power to bring the smell and feel of Easy to life. But Ellis had distracted her, and she had to admit she'd forgotten all about the ring until she realized it was lost.

And now Easy was standing in front of her, true flesh and blood. But it just felt . . . too late.

She looked into Easy's confused and worried face. "I'll always love you." Her words came out all warbled, and it killed her to look at Easy's crushed blue eyes. But she had to say it. She put her hand on his chest and wished she felt differently, but just as she'd been so sure just months ago that she loved him more than anything—now she was sure that it was over. "But I think it's over." She bit her tongue to keep from saying that she'd spent the last ten hours not thinking about him—and still having a great time.

"Callie." Easy coughed into his fist. "Did I do something? I'm so sorry I haven't been able to call or . . ."

Callie stared straight up, up at the glowing tower of the Empire State Building in the black night sky. Snow fell harder and harder, landing on her eyelashes and blurring her sight. She shook her head slowly and stepped backward, away from Easy. "It's all right. It's better this way. It just is." She raised her hand and turned around, surprised at how easy it was to turn away from him. He remained standing by the guardrail without saying a word.

She wondered if she should hug him, or tell him they could always be friends, but anything she had to say seemed meaningless now. With a deep breath, she stepped back into the elevator. And as the doors closed, she let the tears fall.

28

A WAVERLY OWL KNOWS THAT THE MIDDLE OF THE NIGHT ISN'T ALWAYS THE DARKEST HOUR.

Tinsley drifted in and out of sleep as the black night sky over the city slowly turned a milky gray. After the hot tub portion of the party had disbanded, everyone had huddled around the giant fireplace in Yvonne's living room, telling ghost stories under blankets until people started falling asleep. She'd tucked Jenny safely into one of the guest beds, but she just couldn't fall asleep. Her nerves were still on edge thinking about the look Julian had shot her when she'd bossily escorted the drunken Jenny from the hot tub. After the last whispers had quieted, she'd tossed and turned for hours. Finally she'd grabbed a lime green North Face sleeping bag, made a cup of hot cocoa, and was sitting out on the roof deck, leaning against the brick wall of Yvonne's building and staring out at the beautiful, snowy pre-dawn. Alone.

Her giant ceramic mug of watery instant hot chocolate

cooled in her palms. She blew into the mug, the steam rising and drifting out toward the shadowy rooftops across Park Avenue. Tinsley loved climbing onto her own roof at her parents' place and had a secret compartment under one of the vents to stash her cigarettes and the occasional pilfered joint.

God, her Thanksgiving weekend had sucked. First her parents had ditched her without notice—she had to remember to still be pissed about that the next time she spoke to her mom—and then she'd momentarily reconciled with Julian, only to have that mega-bitch Sleigh ruin everything. Tinsley wasn't going to get another chance.

Eventually, the sun popped up over the East River, casting the city in shadow. The Empire State Building looked huge and intimidating. She couldn't really believe Callie had dumped Easy—when Callie had come back to Yvonne's late last night, tear-streaked and a little shaky, she'd spilled everything. It was all for the best, really. Tinsley thought of her words of advice to Jenny—*relax, have fun. Don't start planning your wedding.* She meant them, really she did . . . but she knew what it was like, too, to meet someone who completely changed your life.

It was Julian's loss, she reminded herself for the millionth time. How could he be so easily taken in by Sleigh? He was only a freshman, but *still.* How could he not see what a transparent little bitch she was? Tinsley fumbled for her cigarettes and lit one up, blowing a torrent of smoke into the crisp air.

The door to the roof opened and Tinsley's spirits sank

further—if she had to watch some of Jeremy's friends come out to watch the sunrise and mack on high school girls, she'd puke. A foot kicked the door when it stuck, just like Tinsley had had to do, and Julian peeked around the corner, his dirty blond hair matted down in an appealing case of bed-head. He didn't look surprised to see her, which agitated Tinsley even more.

"What now?" she asked haughtily. "Are you going to criticize me for yelling at a drunk girl?" She didn't mean to sound like such a bitch, but since he thought she was one anyway, what difference did it make?

Julian had that hazy look of someone who'd just woken up. "No," he said, his voice almost a whisper. "May I?"

Tinsley shrugged, pulling her sleeping bag further over her shoulders, like a protective fleece cocoon. "Help yourself."

Julian righted a plastic chair, wiping his hand across the seat before gingerly sitting down. He was wearing his jeans with a borrowed black Columbia sweatshirt, and its sleeves were a little too short. "Actually, that was a nice thing you did for Jenny," he said, clearing his throat to vanquish his morning voice.

Tinsley eyed him cautiously. "Thanks." She sipped her hot chocolate, which had gone cold in her hand. She choked back the swallow so as not to spit it back into her mug. "But I'll never be as nice as Sleigh, apparently."

"Yeah, about her . . ." Julian smiled sheepishly, running his bare hand through his hair and making it even messier.

"What about her?" Tinsley tried to conceal her annoyance. The last thing she wanted to do was talk about Sleigh, and she was sorry she'd mentioned the bitch's name. If he was going to tell her that Sleigh was coming back to Waverly, or that they were dating, Tinsley would have to hurl something off the roof of the building—possibly her own body.

"When I was talking to her after dinner, it came up that you and I had, you know, hooked up before." Julian's cheeks flushed a little as he said this. He kicked at the snow with his sneakers, his feet bare inside them. "And she sort of freaked out on me."

"Really?" Tinsley sipped again at her cold cocoa, trying to keep the joy from her voice. She resisted asking if Sleigh had tried to throw all his shit out the window—even she knew better than to gloat.

Julian nodded. "I always sensed there was something a little off about her. I just couldn't put my finger on what exactly it was." He leaned over and traced his fingers in the snow, scooping up a thin layer and tossing it into the air. "My best friend at home had this girlfriend who was all sweet and charming, and once we were hanging out late down at the beach and he forgot to call her and she came screaming down in this little powder blue Volkswagen bug—she didn't even have her driver's license. The shit that came out of her mouth freaked everyone out. And none of us saw it coming."

"Hmm," Tinsley said, rocking back and forth for warmth. She was suddenly aware that her leg was falling asleep. "So you're saying you're a poor judge of character?"

"Not always." Julian stuffed his hands into the pockets of his jeans. "I sensed Sleigh had that in her somewhere. Guess I was right."

Tinsley wrinkled her nose. "If you suspected she was a bitch, why were you all BFF with her?"

"I just wanted to see how you'd act around her," he admitted. "Sorry."

A gust of wind kicked up and Julian rubbed his hands together and blew into them. Tinsley glanced at him and then looked off into the distance, her mind racing. He'd just been testing her? Why? He would only do that if . . . well, if he were interested. Again. "I thought we were done playing games with each other," she couldn't resist adding.

Julian laughed, then stared straight down at Tinsley, his eyes like lasers. "I guess I'm not perfect either."

"So . . ." Tinsley trailed off.

Julian shrugged. "I'd like to try hanging out again. If you're into it."

Tinsley gave a small smile. "I'd like that," she agreed. "My parents are out of town, so I'm headed back to Waverly tomorrow. Or later today, I mean. Are you . . . spending the whole weekend with Kevin?"

Julian yawned, covering his mouth with his fingers. The yawn transformed into a smile. "Now that I've missed out on the turkey, I might as well head back too. Want company on the train?"

"Always." Tinsley smiled back. She'd managed to regain the feeling in her leg.

"Cool." Julian yawned again. "I gotta get some more sleep. Don't stay up here too long—you'll freeze to death."

Tinsley nodded and watched as Julian wrestled with the roof

door again and then disappeared inside. She looked out over the horizon that had seemed so bleak before the sun rose, and before Julian's visit. Now, with the orangey-pink sun rising up behind the tall, elegant gray buildings, it felt like a brand-new day. So, Julian hadn't exactly professed his undying love for her.

Yet.

 **OwlNet**

CallieVernon: I broke up w/ EZ.

BrettMesserschmidt: What? How did you even talk to him? Isn't he still in his barracks? Aren't you in Atlanta?

CallieVernon: He went AWOL to visit me in NYC. Long story . . . but I realized I wasn't ready to be so serious.

BrettMesserschmidt: Aw, sweetie. You sound sad.

CallieVernon: I am. But it's 4 the best. I'm flying home today. My mom wants to talk about the whole accidentally-sending-me-to-rehab thing.

BrettMesserschmidt: She'd better take you makeup shopping!

CallieVernon: Ha. Retail therapy is an essential part of the healing process.

29

A WAVERLY OWL NEVER KISSES AND TELLS—UNLESS HE'S TRYING TO PROVE HE ISN'T GAY.

Bright, almost blinding sunlight glittered across the snow-covered Waverly grounds as Brandon and Heath trudged back across campus over the unplowed paths sometime after seven on Friday morning. The cold winter wind whipped through their clothes, but Brandon couldn't feel a thing. He grinned at Heath and Heath grinned back.

"Man, that was excellent." Brandon fumbled through his pocket for his black Gucci aviators. "Just what the doctor ordered."

"Dr. Heath always delivers." Heath whinnied and did a quick gallop around Brandon before holding out his gloved hand for a high five. Brandon slapped it hard.

Brandon couldn't remember the last time he'd stayed up all night—if ever. He'd heard about all-night parties growing up, but he'd never been invited to any, so the idea had acquired the status of myth in his mind. Making out with Helga—he was ninety percent sure it had been Helga, not Gretchen—had been well worth the wait, though. He couldn't believe how easily it had all come to him. Was it possible Heath was rubbing off on him?

Just thinking about it put a bounce in his step, and he slowed so that Heath could keep up.

"You gonna see Gretchen again before they leave?" Brandon asked as they slushed through a puddle. The snow-covered spire of Waverly's chapel appeared in the distance.

Heath shrugged. "Doubtful," he answered, rewrapping his cranberry and beige Burberry scarf around his neck.

"Why not?" Brandon asked. Helga had begged him to sneak back before she had to leave on Sunday, and while he wasn't sure the date required Heath's presence, he didn't want to make the trek alone and somehow get stuck talking to Dunderdorf about goats again.

"Don't get me wrong." Heath puffed up. They turned up the path toward Richards, passing a couple of international students making snow angels on the smooth white Commons. "We totally clicked."

"But?"

"But we just cuddled," Heath admitted, stuffing his hands into the pockets of his coat. "Which is still cool."

Brandon couldn't believe his ears. The self-proclaimed lothario had spent the entire night . . . cuddling? Wait, did that make Brandon more pimp than Heath? "Sure," Brandon said, rethinking how smooth Helga's skin had felt, like in Switzerland they somehow had some miracle kind of moisturizer that turned skin into silk. "It's cool." *But I'm cooler.*

"I just kept . . ." Heath's voice trailed off. He kicked a big clump of snow into the air. "You know. Thinking about Kara."

Brandon stopped in his tracks. He knew Heath had been crushed when Kara dumped him the month before—he'd never seen his roommate actually cry before, and it was touching, in a freaky kind of way. But after a few days of moping around, Heath had managed nearly effortlessly to slip back into his old wisecracking, panty-chasing self. Or so Brandon had thought. He looked at Heath, whose normally carefree eyes confirmed what he was saying. He wasn't over Kara.

"Are you going to tell her?" Brandon asked, curious. Now that he thought about it, it *had* seemed strange when Heath was unnaturally interested in seeing the Theater Club's showing of *A Midsummer Night's Dream* last week. Brandon had assumed it had more to do with the rumor that the forest nymphs were naked than the fact that Kara Whalen was listed as the stage manager, but now he had to rethink things.

"I don't know, dude," Heath said, mildly annoyed, or just pretending to be. He kept walking. "It's just a fact. Not sure there's anything to be done about it."

Brandon patted him on the back. Heath knocked Brandon into a snowbank in retaliation. "Not so fast, motherfucker!" The boys chased each other all the way back to their dorm, pelting each other with the hardest snowballs they could make.

A WAVERLY OWL ALWAYS SAYS GOODBYE.

Tinsley appeared in the breakfast nook of Yvonne Stidder's apartment early Friday morning, dropping her Prada bag at her feet. "Hello, can we get moving, please?" she moaned cheerfully, plopping herself down on Callie's lap.

"Someone's in a good mood." Callie sat with an uneaten toasted bagel smeared with grape jelly still in front of her. She tried to twist out from under Tinsley's lithe body, but Tinsley just wrapped an arm around Callie's neck and planted a kiss on her cheek.

"A *very* good mood," Jenny noted, staring miserably at the crumbs of her orange and cranberry muffin. She wasn't quite sure she'd seen Tinsley look happy before. Ever. She'd seen her look satisfied, smarmy, gloating, devilish, cheerful, even content, but not happy. Her purply-blue Elizabeth Taylor eyes positively sparkled.

Jenny didn't feel nearly as good, suffering from a severe

hangover and a case of intense regret. She hadn't seen Casey
again after drunkenly saying she was in love with him, and
every time she thought about it, she wanted to throw up. All
over again. She'd made a complete fool of herself over a guy
she hardly knew—again. She took another huge gulp of water
and hoped the four extra-strength Advils would start to kick
in soon.

Tinsley arched a dark, perfectly shaped eyebrow. Her smooth
black hair was pulled back into two damp ponytails that started
at the nape of her neck and hung halfway down her short-sleeved
black and gray striped Juicy Couture cardigan. "I guess I'm just
ready to get back to school." She took a bite out of Callie's bagel
before hopping up and brushing the sesame seeds off her dark
Rock & Republic skirt.

"I wonder why." Callie twisted the corners of her pouty,
Chanel-glossed lips into a half-smile. She picked at a glob of
jelly that had landed on her pink Ralph Lauren turtleneck and
tilted her head toward the living room, where Julian was collapsed on the couch, playing video games.

"Are you really going back?" Jenny stuffed her plate in the
stainless steel sink overloaded with dishes and remnants of food.
She'd offered, halfheartedly, to help Yvonne clean up today, but
Yvonne had cheerfully promised that the cleaning crew were
scheduled to arrive in a few hours and were looking forward to
the bonus holiday weekend pay. "You're welcome at my house
now that the Hare Krishnas have evacuated."

"That's sweet." Tinsley, in a pair of dark gray ribbed tights,
spun around in a circle on her toe. "But I'm all set."

"What about you?" Jenny asked Callie, whose hazel eyes had been looking a little dazed all morning. Callie pushed her bagel away from her and stood up.

"I changed my plane ticket." Callie's shirt rose to reveal a tiny strip of pale white skin above her black Sevens. "I'm going home. For down time."

"Need a little home cooking?" Tinsley asked, rubbing her stomach teasingly. "Some grits and cornbread?"

"Something like that." Callie stuck out her tongue. "My mom has a fuckload of making up to do." She tossed her wavy strawberry-blond hair and shrugged. "That should be good for a new pair of Louboutins, at least."

"You ready?" Julian asked, poking his head into the kitchen. In a faded gray plaid shirt over a Raconteurs T-shirt, and a pair of saggy jeans, his hair damp and falling in a million different directions, he looked totally adorable. Jenny glanced over at Tinsley, who had definitely noticed his cuteness too.

A smile twitched at the corners of Tinsley's glossed lips. "Julian's taking the train back too."

Callie and Jenny exchanged glances, and Tinsley wrinkled her nose at them before Julian could see.

"Let me get my bag—I'll walk down with you." Callie disappeared in a swirl of Joy Jean Patou perfume.

Jenny wandered through the apartment, still slightly depressed, glancing around for anything she might have left behind. Casey had disappeared some time early that morning. Without saying goodbye. Jenny tried not to let it bother her, instead thinking about how nice it would be to spend a few days with her dad—and just her dad. Maybe they'd wander through the bookstores on the Upper West Side, trolling for treasures and doing a little early Christmas shopping. They'd stop and have lunch at one of Jenny's favorite soup places, or the hole-in-the wall Thai place down the block that made the best pad Thai she'd ever tasted.

Moments later she stepped out of the elevator with Tinsley and Callie and Julian. The cold morning air felt crisp and fresh as the doorman opened the door for them. They stood under the building's forest green canopy and fumbled for their sunglasses. The glittering snowbanks hadn't had time to get all grimy and gray yet, and the city looked like a winter wonderland. Jenny's heart raced. She loved being home.

"We need a cab," Tinsley said, bumping her bag against Julian's as she dropped it to the sidewalk.

"Three, actually." Callie looked up at the sky, and Jenny wondered if she was looking for the Empire State Building, and wondering if Easy was still there. She'd told them all the whole story this morning, and Jenny kind of wished she could give Easy a hug. She knew what it was like to have her heart broken—or maybe she didn't. Had she ever really been in love?

"Where are you going?" the doorman asked, overhearing.

"Grand Central," Julian told him. He picked up Tinsley's bag for her and brought it over to the curb.

"JFK." Callie pulled on a pair of baby blue cashmere gloves.

"Upper West Side," Jenny said.

The doorman flipped his whistle out from under his vest and stepped out onto Park Avenue, thrusting his hand in the air.

Jenny's phone buzzed in her pocket and she grabbed it instinctively, almost dropping it in the snow. She saw an unfamiliar number, which always panicked her, but she opened it anyway. *Hey I'm sorry I didn't get to say goodbye. U looked 2 cute asleep. UR sweet and you should totally come visit me at Union. Xo. Casey.*

"It's not the Hare Krishnas, is it?" Tinsley asked, a look of mock alarm on her face.

"What Hare Krishnas?" Julian asked, confused.

"I'll tell you later." Tinsley casually put her glove on his arm. "It's a story for the train."

"It's Casey." Jenny excitedly read the text aloud, the words tripping off her tongue proudly.

"Someone has a new boyfriend," Callie said nonchalantly, staring down at the toes of her boots.

"Mmm, maybe not." Jenny snapped her phone shut, feeling empowered. Maybe she'd text him back later . . . or wait until tomorrow. Or maybe she wouldn't text him at all. "I don't know if I'm ready for a boyfriend right now."

As soon as the words left her lips, Jenny knew that they were true. Since she'd first met Casey, all she'd wanted was for him to want her. And now that he did, well . . . maybe it was more fun not to be attached to anyone. For now.

Tinsley grinned at Jenny, a silent congratulations between them. Jenny smiled back.

Forget the man of her dreams. Right now, all she wanted was to have a little more fun.

A WAVERLY OWL IS NEVER TOO PROUD TO BEG.

"Turn left here," Brett instructed, squinting at the printed out Mapquest directions. "Then turn right in point two miles."

"He really lives here?" Bree asked, turning the wheel of her rental BMW Mini. It was Sunday afternoon, and Bree was on her way back to New York. Willy, who had spent the rest of the weekend hanging out with the Messerschmidts, had insisted on taking the train back, to give Bree and Brett a little alone time. It was totally sweet of him, and on the ride up through New Jersey, Brett had spilled the whole drama-filled tale of her past few months at Waverly, from hooking up with Mr. Dalton, the hot but slimy Latin teacher, to hooking up with Kara, to breaking up with Jeremiah—three times. Bree had laughed at the right spots and said exactly the kind of sisterly things Brett knew she'd say, and she already felt one thousand times better.

"Here!" Brett cried out. "Twelve-twelve Eastman Parkway. This is it." Brett took in the manicured green lawn and the enormous Tudor mansion. Her heart skipped a beat at the sight of the black Mustang, trunk open, still in the driveway. "Thanks for the ride, B." Brett gave her sister a long hug.

"Love ya, sis." Bree glanced over the top of her red aviators. "Be good." Brett grabbed her bag from the backseat and waved as the Mini shot back down the driveway. With a deep breath, Brett turned and headed up the paved driveway toward the steps. But before she could reach them, the dark oak Old English door—with a giant iron lion's head as a knocker—opened and Sebastian came out, leather jacket on, collar up.

He stopped when he saw Brett. "What are you doing here?"

Brett's face flushed. She hadn't exactly thought out what she was going to say, and suddenly it seemed like a bad idea to just, like, show up. "I wanted to, uh, take you up on your offer. Of a ride back to Waverly." She shuffled her feet.

Sebastian tilted his head and stared at Brett for a second before shrugging his shoulders. "Whatever." A giant red and blue Tommy Hilfiger bag was slung over his shoulder, and he pulled the door shut behind him, then tugged it to make sure it was locked.

Sliding into the passenger seat, Brett primly tugged at the hem of her black and white geometric-print miniskirt, but for once, Sebastian didn't even glance at her legs. Disappointed, she stared straight out the window.

"Your house looks nice," she offered. She wondered if it had some faux-English motifs inside, or a billiards room, but as she opened her mouth to ask, Sebastian spoke up.

"You can pick the station," he offered, cautiously pulling out of the driveway. Brett kind of missed the way he usually gunned it.

"That's okay," Brett deferred. "It's your car."

"Really, it's cool." He didn't even glance at her. "Whatever you want is fine with me."

Brett fiddled with the radio, plowing through the static to find a station not on a commercial. "So, uh . . . you ready to go back?" she asked awkwardly as Sebastian pulled onto the freeway.

Sebastian shrugged. "Yeah." His black Hugo track jacket with white stripes down the sides looked brand-new. Maybe his family gave Thanksgiving presents, or maybe he'd hit up the Mall at Short Hills on Friday, too. "You?"

Brett fiddled with the multi-stranded turquoise neck-lace around her neck. What was wrong with him? She hated to admit it, but she missed the playful tone of their previous car rides and knew it was her fault. The notion that she owed him an apology for what had happened at Thanksgiving was nagging her. It wasn't cool to use him as some kind of pawn in a game to annoy the Coopers, and it was even less cool to have a screaming match with her sister about it. But bringing it up again would be so . . . awkward.

"Yeah, I guess," she replied, her voice equally casual.

They merged into the heavy traffic, cars loaded down with

families headed home after the long weekend break. A sea of red taillights sprawled out in front of them as cars stopped and started again in the traffic jam.

They sat in silence for a while, until Brett couldn't take it anymore. "Did you have a good time with your family?"

"Sure." Sebastian nodded, humming along to the radio. He cracked open the window and lit a cigarette. The smell of smoke and Sebastian's cologne mingled in her nose and she was surprised at how comforting the smell was, reminding her of the last couple of days at home. With the elder Coopers cleared out, her parents and sister had reverted to their normal selves. They'd made a pact to behave in front of Bree's future in-laws—that's what they were calling them—without going overboard. Last night, Willy had come over to watch cable, surfing from reality show to reality show while eating giant bowls of Cherry Garcia ice cream. Bree and Brett gave each other manicures while Willy tried to teach Peaches and Princess to play dead. Though the long weekend had begun stressfully, Brett felt totally revived, ready to head back to the insanity that was Waverly.

But still there was something nagging at her. She hadn't exactly been thinking about Sebastian all weekend, but his lively presence had left an aura in her house and random thoughts about him—how much the Teacups loved him, how pleased he'd been when he remembered her from the shore from so many summers ago—had popped into her mind. And she hadn't hated it.

"Look." Brett shifted in her seat and bit her Dior Addict

Red Stockings–glossed lips. "I owe you an apology," she said stiffly.

Sebastian cocked his head but kept his eyes on the road.

Brett realized how stupid she sounded and dropped into her regular voice. "No really, I'm sorry."

"For what?" Sebastian asked. He slowed the car to maintain the flow of traffic. The brake lights in front of them fluttered on and off and then remained a solid red. Sebastian stopped the car and they sat, trapped in gridlock. The skyline of New York was visible off in the distance.

"I'm sorry for inviting you to Thanksgiving under false pretenses." Brett stared down at her freshly painted red nails.

"To embarrass me," Sebastian added. She could still hear the hurt in his voice.

"Is that what you think? That I wanted to *embarrass* you?" She'd never want to intentionally cause someone pain—and definitely not Sebastian.

He shrugged again. "You clearly didn't invite me over because you wanted to hang out with me."

"I'll admit I had ulterior motives." She twisted toward him in her seat. It was stupid of her not to realize it sooner, but she'd had a really great time hanging out with Sebastian, completely independent of the Coopers, and it suddenly was really important to her that he understood that. "I wanted to, you know, kind of shock those sticks-in-the-mud." She looked up at him, chagrined. "But I ended up having a lot of fun with you. Can you just, you know, forgive me?"

Sebastian narrowed his eyes. "Yeah, I guess," he said, cracking a half-smile. "It's not like I didn't enjoy the look on that old broad's face when you caught her staring at my hair."

"She dug it—I know she did," Brett assured him, laughing. She glanced out the corner of her eye at him and sighed, turning serious again. "I'm not particularly proud of my behavior. It's just that my sister was—"

Sebastian held out his hand. "Hey, it's over." He glanced at her as traffic started to move again. "What's done is done."

"Okay," she said meekly. She stared out the window, wondering if Jenny and Callie were on their way back to Waverly right now. Maybe Jenny would be in when Brett got there, and they could make margaritas. She'd gotten e-mails from her and Callie, filling her in on their crazy breaks, but she couldn't wait to see them in person.

"I just have one question for you." Sebastian rubbed his hand across his face, and Brett tensed up, wondering if it had all been a setup to pay her back for her awful behavior. "Did you pack that sexy outfit you were wearing at Thanksgiving?" He arched his eyebrows and smiled.

Brett felt her whole face blush. She had, in fact, gone through her closet and packed some of her old clothes, the kind that would shock people like the Coopers—but there was no way she was giving Sebastian the satisfaction of knowing that.

"I guess you'll just have to wait and see."

A commercial on the radio faded and a Springsteen song

filtered through the airwaves. Instead of cringing, Brett reached down and turned up the volume, smiling at Sebastian. He grinned back at her and pulled onto the left-hand shoulder, blowing past the stalled traffic as they hurtled toward Waverly's snow-covered grounds.

 OwlNet   Instant Message Inbox

AlanStGirard: Whoa, is it true you hooked up with the Dunderdorf twins???

BrandonBuchanan: Dude, how'd you hear that already?

AlanStGirard: So it's true?

BrandonBuchanan: Not really . . . just one of them.

AlanStGirard: Oh, man! You rock. What about Sage?

BrandonBuchanan: Who??

BennyCunningham: Just saw Brett climbing out of her little study buddy's black sports car.

SageFrancis: Interesting. Were they working on Latin all during break??

BennyCunningham: And I just saw Tinsley curled up on a couch in Maxwell next to that hot frosh, Julian.

SageFrancis: Man, was everyone getting busy over break except me?

BennyCunningham: Now that U mention it, I heard something about Brandon and a Swedish model??

SageFrancis: Thanks. You're like the eighth person to tell me.

 **Owl** Net

EmilyJenkins: Did you hear Callie and EZ are split for good? He was, like, ready to jump off the Empire State bldg or something.

AlisonQuentin: Totally insane! I think me and Alan are kaput now, too.

EmilyJenkins: Oh, no! Need a shoulder to cry on?

AlisonQuentin: More like a stiff drink. And a serious gossip session. Did you hear Jenny and Tinsley are like BFFs now? Word is they're set to stir up some major trouble.

EmilyJenkins: What *happened* over break?

AlisonQuentin: Um, what didn't?

Anna Percy, Cammie Sheppard, and Sam
Sharpe ruled the A-LIST. But there are three
new princesses in Tinseltown.

THE A-LIST
HOLLYWOOD ROYALTY

Meet the new Hollywood Royalty:
Amelie, the not-so-innocent starlet;
Myla and Ash, the golden couple;
Jacob, the geek turned hottie;
and Jojo, the outsider who'll
do anything to get on the A-List.

**SOME PEOPLE ARE
BORN WITH IT.**

Turn the page for a sneak peek of
this scandalous new novel by *New York Times*
bestselling author Zoey Dean.

THE FAIRY PRINCESS OF HOLLYWOOD

Amelie Adams's white stretch limo pulled to a stop outside Nokia Theater, where a ruby-red carpet wound its way past the Staples Center and up to the theater's doors. Standing on risers on either side were models wearing hot pink Prada sunglasses and bright white tent dresses with graphic prints of LA landmarks on them: the Hollywood sign, Mann's Chinese Theatre, the Beverly Hills Hotel, a postcard shot of Malibu. At ground level were throngs of fans, hoping for a glimpse of their favorite Hollywood starlets arriving for the premiere of *The A-List*.

"Fairy Princess!"

"Fairy Princess!"

Even though Amelie wasn't in the movie, her fans knew she was coming tonight. Through the limo's tinted glass, she saw clusters of little girls waving homemade, glittery signs proclaiming their love for her character. Amelie leaned back in her seat, pushing a red ringlet from her Tiffany–box–blue eyes.

Her mother's face broke into the wide, full-lipped smile that Amelie had inherited. Helen Adams's own red hair was shorter and her eyes were a dark hazel, but otherwise she and Amelie could have been mistaken for sisters.

"Have fun. And remember, you'll get it next time." She

winked one heavily-made-up eye.

Amelie's shell-pink lips formed a grimace. She'd been up for the part of Emma Hardy, *The A-List*'s lead, but lost the role to a just-discovered blonde the producers deemed "more mature." The Emma character had a sex scene, and while Amelie knew that a jump from petting winged ponies to heavy petting would've been a risky career move, sometimes she longed to do *something* that wasn't G-rated.

"Fairy Princess! Fairy Princess!"

Amelie stepped out of the limousine, plastering on the same grin that had sold four million T-shirts with her face on it. Her new Miu Miu wedges sunk into the crimson carpet and she gracefully adjusted the hem of her silver Jovani flapper-inspired dress. Her character wore pink exclusively, so it was nice to not feel like human cotton candy for once.

She made her way down the row of screaming fans, signing pictures, posters, and BOP magazines in her trademark swirly script. After each autograph, she flourished her pink Sharpie with Fairy Princess's signature wand-wave.

At the far end of the red carpet, cast members from *The A-List* mingled with other actors about her age. Raven-haired Kady Parker and Moira and Deven Lacey, twins who just got parts on *School of Scandal*, a new CW show, shot her curious glances and then returned to their conversation.

Amelie sighed, signing a talking Fairy Princess doll with bubblegum pink hair and glittery accessories. She knew she was lucky to be seated at the helm of a multi-million dollar empire at only sixteen, but sometimes she just wanted to move up from the kids' table. She was growing up, but no one besides Mary Ellen, the on-set stylist who had to let her Fairy Princess wardrobe out in the chest, had really seemed to notice.

Amelie smiled at a white-blond seven-year-old in a replica of Fairy Princess's Winter Festival ballgown. She handed Amelie a shirt to sign. "Is it true you're playing a new kind of fairy in *Class Angel*?" the little girl asked.

"You got it," Amelie answered. Filming started tomorrow on the new Kidz Network movie *Class Angel*. It was PG, and more mature than her Fairy Princess role, but she still played a teenager's guardian angel rather than an *actual* teenager. It was like calling Pinkberry ice cream.

Amelie laid the shirt on one of the models' platforms, crouching in front of the little girl.

"Mommy!" The little girl pointed at Amelie, then yelled, "Mom, Fairy Princess has boobies!"

Amelie felt the blood rush to her face faster than West-siders hit The Grove during a Barney's Co-op sale. Well then. Maybe people *were* noticing her growing up, after all. . . .

THE REAL PRINCESS OF HOLLYWOOD

Myla Everhart stood in the LAX baggage claim, wishing she hadn't worn her Pucci Sundial dress—every time she sat down, the back of her legs touched some invariably sticky surface. The first daughter of America's hottest on- and off-screen couple craned her neck, looking toward the doors to the street. Ash had said he'd park and come inside to help her with her bags. Granted, she'd internationally overnighted her bags via Luggage Concierge, but he could certainly carry her plum Marc Jacobs tote full of French *Vogues* and her cashmere travel blanket.

Myla fished her emerald-adorned iPhone from the bottom of her bag. 1:14. Ash knew she landed at 12:30. What was the freaking holdup?

But then . . . that was Ash. Her Ash. Laid-back, easygoing, Ash.

She softened just thinking of him. Long before they got together, Ash Gilmore was her best friend and the only guy who *got* Myla. It wasn't easy going through puberty as the child of Barkley Everhart and Lailah Barton—*People's* Most Beautiful Couple, 2001, 2002, 2006–present. Most inattentive, too, by Myla's standards. They'd adopted Myla as a baby, after spending time on-set in Thailand, filming an Adam and Eve–inspired love story that grossed some ungodly amount. It had been just Myla, until they brought home Mahalo from Bangladesh on her twelfth birthday. They'd just returned from a *Babel*-meets-*Independence Day* shoot and decided to bring back a souvenir. At least that's how it seemed to Myla.

Then one day in the eighth grade, she was stranded after school because her driver was late to pick her up. Ash was waiting for his dad, Gordon Gilmour, a record producer who spent more time coddling whiny rock stars than taking care of his son. She and Ash were like two lost souls, who both happened to be extremely photogenic. Myla was in the middle of a rant about how Mahalo had gotten to choose his own bedroom furniture when Ash leaned over and kissed her, right there on the stairs of their middle school parking lot. They'd been Hollywood's youngest Golden Couple ever since, and were always together.

But Myla's parents—Barbar, as they were called by the press—had insisted on a family vacation this summer. "Vacation" meant a whirlwind tour of the Third World, doing United Nations aid work at their adopted countries: Thailand for Myla, Bangladesh for Mahalo and Madagascar for Bobby. Myla had to share a room with her two brothers, often in villages so small and remote she couldn't get a cell phone signal or Internet. She couldn't indulge in online retail therapy, update her Facebook status, or, more importantly, communicate with Ash. It was *torture*.

Granted, she could have called Ash every second while she was in Paris last week, visiting her old friend Isabelle, whom she hadn't seen since fourth grade. But she'd been in the City of Love without the love of her life—thinking about him too much would have depressed her.

Myla punched a string of numbers into her phone, twirling a lock of her long ebony hair around her index finger. She smiled, catching a glimpse of the shiny, emerald-green streak that fell along the left side of her neck. It had been Ash's idea, and Myla had initially been revolted, but now she loved the secret burst of color.

Isabelle picked up on the third ring. *"Ma chère amie,* I missed you, too."

Myla could hear the clinking of silverware and wineglasses

in the background. Even though it was after eleven there, Isabelle was probably just eating dinner now, before hitting Paris's nightclubs.

"Stop that, Guillaume!" Isabelle squealed delightedly to her boyfriend. "Sorry, he's being a total perv. Shouldn't you be with Ash?"

"He's late." Myla fiddled nervously with the Green Lantern bubblegum machine ring she wore on a Tiffany gold chain. She and Ash had traded rings from a Cracker Jack box in eighth grade, and she had worn the plastic jewelry on her neck ever since. Myla fully planned to hire Mindy Weiss, the best wedding planner in L.A., to work the cheap rings into the ceremony when they got married.

"Better he's late than you are, if you know what I mean," Isabelle said bawdily, before cracking up. "Oh, that's right! You haven't done it yet. *C'est dommage.*"

Myla rolled her eyes. "We can't all be French sluts like you," she teased her friend.

A woman in a JESUS SAVES (ASK ME HOW) T-shirt rumbled by, scowling at the dirty talk.

"I know, you're waiting for the right time," Isabelle yawned. "Just make sure to take advantage of being young and hot. Now go moisturize before he gets there."

Isabelle hung up with a giggle, probably to stop Guillaume's wandering hands again, and Myla flipped off her phone. Two girls walked by arm in arm, wearing matching Fairy Princess T-shirts and glittery purple leggings.

Myla sighed. Even if they were only ten, you had to start learning fashion *sometime.* She yanked the pile of dog-eared *Vogue*s from her bag and thrust the magazines into the taller girl's arms.

If thoughts of "stranger danger" occurred to either girl, they didn't show it. They studied Myla's round cheeks, smooth skin, and almond-shaped, shamrock-colored eyes. A flash of recognition flashed across their pink-hued faces. They must have seen her photo in *People*, helping Barbar hand out care packages in the Philippines. And here she was again, doing charity work of her own.

Ash Gilmour was late for everything, a habit he'd never wanted to develop but learned from his father, record impresario Gordon Gilmour. "Early means eager. Eager is weak," he'd always said.

But when it came to Myla Everheart, Ash *was* weak. And he'd wanted to be waiting at LAX when she'd landed. He wanted to watch her come down the escalator to the baggage claim, to see whatever impossible shoes she was wearing, followed by her long legs with the tiny birthmark below her right knee. Then her slim little body, and her tumble of hair with the green streak just for him. And then that face—lips that reminded him of the cherries on top of a sundae and eyes that always looked a little sleepy but saw every little thing.

Ash parked his black Mini Cooper and stumbled out, half running across the wide one-way street reserved for shuttle buses and taxis. He dashed past planters of daisies lining the median and skidded to a stop. On the drive over, he'd called House of Petals to get Myla's favorite hot pink peony bouquet, but they were crazed with some Endeavor agent's wedding. He reached down and picked six daisies, then sprinted across the rest of the street, nearly getting hit by a limo driver.

Safely on the sidewalk, Ash composed himself and stepped through the automatic doors. The air conditioning swallowed him, but he saw no sign of Myla on the benches or near the baggage carousel. He checked the arrivals board. Her flight had made it. Had she left without him?

Myla was in the LAX ladies room, applying a final coat of Urban Decay XXX gloss in Baked. Satisfied, she tossed her hair and headed for the door. Surely Ash would be here by *now*.

Swinging her bag back to her shoulder, she pushed through the doors only to be greeted not by her boyfriend but by four paparazzi.

"Myla, where's Barbar?"

Now that Myla was sixteen, and with her parents less, she got photographed more and more on her own. Some days she didn't mind it, but after a fourteen-hour flight? Come on.

She gave the photogs a sarcastic smile, knowing an unflattering scowl would certainly make the tabloids. "Take your pick: Adopting a baby from a war-torn region. Building houses in a hurricane-ravaged stretch of the South. Having wild passionate affairs with their co-stars."

A photographer donning a jet-black goatee asked, "Are they here, Myla? You can tell us." His eyes were focused on Myla's toned thighs.

Myla raised her eyebrows. "First, take a picture, it lasts longer. Which you should already know. Second, no, my parents are not here. Now please get out of my way."

They fired a few more shots and were gone. Myla blinked post-flashbulb into the crowd of new arrivals. And that's when she saw him.

There, clutching a sad bouquet of crumpled daisies, was Ash. His sun-lightened hair hung shaggily over his ears, and his chestnut-colored eyes looked like a heartbroken puppy's. She stopped where she stood, waiting for him to come to her.

Once he spotted her, he nearly tripped over his Vans trying to reach her faster. When he did, he lifted her into the air, dropping the daisies to the polished airport floor. And with hundreds of travelers and tourists surrounding them, he kissed her like it was the only thing he ever needed to be good at in his whole life.

Myla was only vaguely conscious that the paparazzi were shooting photos of them. Their reunion wouldn't make a cover but, because of her parents, they'd get an inset box. She could see the caption now: HOLLYWOOD'S PRINCESS FINDS HER PRINCE CHARMING.

A camera popped several shots right next to their faces. But this time, she wasn't annoyed. In fact, she'd probably have the best one framed.

THE *NEW* PRINCESS OF HOLLYWOOD?

Josephine Milford—Jojo to anyone who wanted to stay on her good side—tossed another Roxy hoodie atop the mountainous pile of clothing in the center of her sustainable bamboo bed. She heaved a sigh, then gathered her thick brown hair into a ponytail at the top of her head. Her room was stuffy, since her parents refused to set the A/C below eighty-four degrees.

Jojo was packing for Greenland, of all places, and she wasn't having an easy go of it. Her wardrobe go-to's—miniskirts, tank tops, lightweight cotton T-shirts, and her most flattering Gap v-neck—didn't exactly scream "ice-bound continent!" Sure, her parents were on their sabbatical from UC Sacramento, but who takes a sixteen-year-old girl to Greenland for her pivotal junior year?

She turned to her mirrored closet door, wondering how she would look after a semester in the snow. Today she was wearing her Sacramento High soccer shorts and a white boys' tank top. Her olive skin, a deep brown thanks to a summer of soccer practice, would probably fade to pale and pasty. Her pink lips would become chapped and wintery. Hopefully, her blue-gray eyes wouldn't freeze shut as she cried away her school year in Greenland's frigid tundra.

Jojo stuck out her tongue at her reflection as she waited

for her best friend, Willa Barnes, to come back to the phone. They were discussing the tragic way Jojo would be spending the next nine months.

"Sorry about that," Willa finally breathed into the phone. "Damian put his turtle in the toilet bowl."

Jojo would babysit Willa's little brother Damian until she turned fifty if it meant she could stay in Sacramento. Not that it was the capital of cool or anything, but it was better than Nuuk. At least she had friends here. Plus, she'd made forward on the soccer team.

"You know that cute miniskirt I bought at Bebe last week?" Jojo looked longingly at her short, red A-line skirt with oversized front pockets. She pulled it on over her soccer shorts and admired her tanned calves in the mirror. "Do you want to adopt it?" she sighed, yanking the skirt off and throwing it into a separate pile on her bed. "I don't think Greenland is miniskirt territory."

Willa laughed. "There might be cute Greenlandian guys who need to see a girl wearing something totally inappropriate."

Jojo flopped onto her bed, picking up the latest *Us Weekly*. Barbar and their kids were on the cover with three Bangladesh villagers. Their oldest daughter wore a green Versace halter and a pair of True Religion cutoffs. Jojo tossed the magazine on her desk with her iPod and a stack of books she'd probably read within the first week of boring Greenland life.

"Besides, maybe it will get globally warmed by the time you get there," Willa reasoned.

"Maybe," Jojo said dubiously. She looked out her window, imagining Justin Klatch, the captain of the boys' soccer team, pulling his blue Scion up in front of the house to appeal to her parents for mercy. He was in love with Jojo and needed her to stay in Sacramento. If they took her away now, he'd become a recluse, not even leaving his house for soccer games. Maybe hearing his teary plea, her parents would relent. . . .

There was a knock at Jojo's door.

"Gotta go." Jojo quickly dropped the phone on her night-stand and picked up a pair of jeans. She was supposed to be packing, not chatting. Pretending to fold them, she yelled, "Come in!" to her dads.

Yes, dads.

Yes, plural.

Frederick and Bradley Milford shuffled into her room, looking like cover models for the Non-Threatening Gay Men Catalog. Even in balmy August, they wore sweater vests. Fred's was a little snug around his potato-sack upper body. Bradley was carrying a cup of his favorite free-trade coffee in a National Public Radio pledge drive mug.

"Hi," Jojo said innocently, gesturing to the pile of to-pack items. "Look at all my progress."

Fred looked at her over the top of his horn-rim glasses. "Jojo, can we have a chat?"

She shoved the pile of clothing from her bed, revealing the organic cotton bedspread. "Go for it."

Fred and Bradley sat and Jojo pulled out her IKEA desk chair. She plopped onto it backwards, resting her chin on the seat back. "What's up? Greenland called and canceled? We're ruining my social life and potential for teenage normalcy in Costa Rica instead?"

"No, this is serious," Fred said, tugging a loose thread on his sweater and admiring his new wedding ring. "Why don't you come sit over here?" He patted the bed between him and Bradley. Fred was short and bald with chocolate skin and a soft cuddly look to him. He always wanted to drop ten pounds, though he'd need to lose fifteen to make any difference.

Bradley, on the other hand, was pale and reedy, with pointy features and a wild tuft of blond hair that couldn't be controlled by even hair gel. Jojo knew this because she had tried.

She rolled her desk chair to the bed and, playing along, smushed herself between her dads. "Really, guys, is this going to be another you're-a-woman-now talk? 'Cause I'm totally cool on the tampon thing."

"We'll just say it, Josephine," he began, running his long fingers along his corduroy shorts. She sat up a little straighter at the use of her full name. Had she gone over her cell phone minutes again?

Bradley took a deep breath, like he was about to run a marathon. "Yourbirthparentsfoundus," he quickly said.

Fred placed his pudgy hand on Jojo's knee. "They've been looking for you for years," he explained. "They were really young when they had you and felt forced to give you up."

Her birth parents? Really young? Looking for her for years? The air around Jojo felt heavy. She stared at Bradley, then turned to face Fred.

"They found us through the adoption agency. We met with them last weekend," Fred went on.

Jojo looked from Fred to Bradley and back again, feeling a mixture of elation and fear. "You guys were at that conference about the future of organic fruit," she told them earnestly. "The one about the bees. You said it was fascinating . . ." she said, leadingly.

Fred's eyes shifted to the ground guiltily.

"You lied?" Jojo asked, her finger gripping her soccer shorts. It was easier to focus on her dads' alibi than the fact that her birth parents had come looking for her. "Wait a second . . . Is this some weird surprise going-away party thing? You'll tell me we're going to meet them and then we'll get over to Sadie's Pizza and all my friends will be there?"

Fred gave Bradley a "This isn't in the Gay Dad's Guide" look.

"You guys are serious," she said slowly. She felt as though there were a strange hole somewhere between her chest and her stomach. "It's for real," she breathed. She tried to picture a different family than her, Fred, and Bradley. Getting a hug from an actual *mom*.

Jojo looked at her dads, who were studying her more

closely than their pet avocado tree after a storm. "So what do they want from me?" she asked hesitantly.

"Well, they can't wait to meet you," Bradley said, playing with the corners of Jojo's *Us Weekly*. "And they're really great."

Jojo reached for her beaten up, stuffed Fozzie Bear. She held it to her chest, squeezing. Parents. Her real parents. The little voice she never listened to got louder. She loved Fred and Bradley more than anything but—a mom? She'd always been a little envious of Willa. Willa's mom baked with her, made her Halloween costumes, took her shopping, and had totally helped Jojo with the whole tampon thing, truth be told.

Now she had her own mom. True, she could be some trash-tastic witch. Maybe she was a reality show contestant who just wanted to meet Jojo for added drama in the season finale. But maybe she was . . . normal?

"What are they like?" She grabbed Fred's pudgy arm, then withdrew it, worried her excitement would hurt her dads' feelings.

Bradley pushed his shock of blond hair down, wearing the same serious expression he wore when he came to Jojo's biology class to talk about deforestation.

Neither spoke, and Jojo couldn't take it. "Are they messed up? Are they in a cult or something? Are they deformed?"

"Actually, they're famous," Fred said carefully, his dark eyes showing no hint of this being a joke.

Jojo squeezed Fozzie. "Like they grew the world's biggest watermelon or something?"

"No, famous like . . ." Bradley pointed to the cover of Jojo's *Us Weekly*. Lailah Barton and Barkley Everheart held hands, fingers intertwined, as they gazed lovingly at poverty-stricken Bangladesh. "Like Barbar famous."

Jojo sprang from the bed, dropping Fozzie Bear and grabbing the magazine. She stared at the impossibly attractive people on the cover.

"No one is Barbar famous," Jojo said, incredulously. "Except Barbar."

"Well that's the thing . . ." Fred grabbed her in a half hug. "That's them."

"Lailah and Barkley are your biological parents." Bradley hugged Jojo's other side, squishing her like a panini. "They thought maybe you could come meet them over the weekend, before we leave. It's a short flight." He pulled an envelope from his back pocket.

Jojo snatched it from Bradley's long fingers. She tore it open, her hands shaking. Inside was a plane ticket, leaving tomorrow to LAX.

First class.

She took one more look at her glamorous family on the cover of *Us*—Barkley, Lailah, and her . . . hmm . . . *sister,* Myla. It was for real, then. The world's most famous couple were her mom and dad.

She grabbed her red miniskirt for the Willa adoption pile. It was all wrong for Greenland, but it would be perfect for Hollywood.

Read the rest of
THE A-LIST: HOLLYWOOD ROYALTY
Available everywhere January 2009

Welcome to Poppy.

A poppy is a beautiful blooming red flower
(like the one on the spine of this book). It is also
the name of the new home of your favorite series.

Poppy takes the real world and makes it
a little funnier, a little more fabulous.

Poppy novels are wild, witty, and inspiring.
They were written just for you.

So sit back, get comfy, and pick a Poppy.

poppy

www.pickapoppy.com

THE A-LIST   gossip girl   THE CLIQUE

SECRETS OF MY
HOLLYWOOD LIFE   the it girl   POSEUR